BEHIND YOU
TALES OF TERROR

BLAIR DANIELS

CONTENTS

The Time Out Doll	1
Has Anyone Seen The "Upside-Down Woman"?	10
I Work At A Nursing Home For Monsters	17
There's Something Wrong With My Husband's Paintings	40
There Are Strange Footprints In The Snow	47
AI Keeps Tagging My Dead Friend In Photos	50
I'm The Custodian For An Elementary School	56
The Head In My Fridge	78
There Is Something Horrible In The Biohazard Waste Bags At My Workplace	101
My Grandma Isn't My Grandma	111
Postpartum Decay	125
Lake Serenity	134
Ouija Board	158
STAY ALERT: Children Walking On Roadway	162
A Thousand Deaths	167
I'm An Animal Control Officer	172
White Noise, Black Screen	194
I Got Lost In A Corn Maze	199
I Work At The Last Blockbuster In The World	216
I Let My Son Use The Copier	244

THE TIME OUT DOLL

It all started a week ago.

Someone put a Time Out Doll at our local playground.

If you're not familiar, they're life-sized dolls that look like children in time out or playing hide and seek. They lean face-first against the wall, hiding their faces with their hands. You only ever see the back of them. Some are handmade, using old kids' clothes, a hat, a wig, and some straw for stuffing.

The first time I saw one at the playground, I thought it was a real kid. So did my five-year-old. He went up to the thing and asked, "Want to play hide and seek?"

It didn't move.

I watched from the bench, fear sinking in. *Why isn't that kid moving?* He, or she—it was hard to tell from the long-ish blond hair and bucket hat—was leaned against the green plastic tunnel that Ryan liked to crawl through. Just *standing* there, totally still.

But as I approached, I saw the plasticky shine of its curly blond hair, the snow-white neck poking out from the shirt's collar. I raised my hand and, slowly, gave it a poke.

It wobbled against the tunnel.

It's a doll.

My stomach dropped. *Is this someone's idea of being cute?* It felt like something an 80-year-old granny would do. The type that likes Precious Moments figurines and buys those hyper-realistic baby dolls. *Or maybe it's a prank.* I could see a group of teenagers leaving it here, just to freak out parents. Maybe they hide in the bushes and film people's reactions and put it on their TikTok, or something.

Either way, it creeped me out. Just standing there, totally still, leaned up against the tunnel like that. Its face lined up perfectly with one of the circular holes cut into the tunnel wall, like it was peering inside.

"What is it?" Ryan asked, staring at it.

"It's a doll. They call them Time Out Dolls, because they look like they're in time out," I replied.

"Oh." Then he got on his hands and knees and, before I could stop him, scooted into the tunnel.

"Ryan—"

"Hi!" he said, his voice echoing in the plastic. "Do you wanna play?"

"Come on—"

"It has no face! Why does it have no face?"

"Come on, get out of there," I said, the uneasiness in my stomach growing.

He finally popped his head out and smiled at me. "Can we make sandcastles?"

"Sure," I replied.

I hated making sandcastles, getting sand all over my jeans. But it was *loads* better than dealing with this creepy doll.

―――――――

A few days later, when we went back to the playground, it was still there.

The after-school crowd was there, running up the jungle gym and racing down the slides. But there was one child that was standing still among the commotion: that stupid doll. It was in the same place as before, leaned against the tunnel.

I whipped around, half-expecting to see some giggling teenagers filming us. But there were only tired zombie parents glued to their phones, chaotic kids racing across the mulch.

I went back to my phone, scrolling through the

news. When I looked up a minute later, the doll was in a different place.

It was now leaned up against the slide, hiding its face against the green plastic.

My heart sank. *One of the kids must've moved it,* I thought. I glanced around, at all the screeching, whooping kids.

Right?

I waved to Ryan, about to go down the slide, and put my phone away. I didn't want to take my eyes off him anymore. He waved back, grinning toothily, his bright yellow hat sticking out among the crowd.

But there is always something to distract us from our kids. Dirty dishes in the sink, unread emails... there's always something tugging at our sleeve, crying for our attention. And for me, today, it was a phone call.

As I answered my client's questions, about the logo and branding images I'd designed for her, my eyes strayed from the playground.

And when I looked back, I couldn't see Ryan anymore.

I dropped the phone and stood up. "Ryan!"

Nothing.

I ran around the side of the playground—and that's when I saw his yellow hat.

Not on Ryan.

On that fucking Time Out Doll.

It was now leaned against the rock-climbing wall. Hands covering its face. Shirt softly rippling in the wind. Blond, shiny curls poking out from *my son's* hat.

My blood ran cold. Animalistic fear pounded through my veins. *This is wrong. So wrong.* I opened my mouth to scream for Ryan—

"We switched hats!"

I whipped around to see Ryan standing there.

Perfectly fine, wearing the doll's bucket hat.

I let out a breath. Sunk to my knees. "Thank God you're okay," I said, voice warbling, pulling him in for a hug.

"I'm okay," he replied, confused. "Can we go on the swings?"

"Okay. But first, let's switch your hats back."

Barely looking at the wretched doll, I reached over and yanked off the yellow hat. "Put its hat back on," I told him, and then we made our way to the swings.

I spent a while there, just pushing him, enjoying the sunny—if cold—spring day. The tension began to melt away. Ryan was safe, and everything was fine.

Eventually, as the sun began to set, we made our way back to the parking lot.

As I mentally thought through the steps of preparing dinner—I needed to cut up some carrots, and did we remember to buy heavy cream?—Ryan tugged at my sleeve.

"Why is it there?"

No.

The doll.

It was now at the edge of the parking lot, leaning against a tree.

"Uh... one of the kids must've moved it out here."

"Why?"

"They probably thought it was funny. C'mon, let's go."

We quickly got in the car and drove home.

That night, I decided we'd go to a different playground for a few days. The doll was freaking me out too much. Yeah, maybe it was irrational, but no one said we had to go to that playground. I'd take him to the one in Edgewood tomorrow.

As I put Ryan's hat away, I noticed several strands of curly blond hair stuck inside. Actually, more than several. I pulled them out, my stomach turning a little, and then threw them in the trash. Then I sat down, settled in, and took a sip of tea.

Just as I was finally relaxing, I heard Ryan's voice upstairs.

"MOM!"

I dropped the cup of tea and ran up the stairs. *"Mom! Mom!"* he continued yelling, fear threading his voice.

I burst into the room.

Ryan was cowering in the corner of his bed, covers up to his neck. "It's in my closet," he whispered.

"... What's in your closet?" I asked, fear pounding through me.

"The doll."

No. It's got to be a nightmare.

I paced towards the closet. The door was ajar, the darkness spilling out of it. With each step my heart sank further. *It can't be... just a nightmare...*

I sucked in a breath and swung the door open.

No.

It wasn't a nightmare.

There, in the darkness, stood the Time Out Doll. It was leaned against the hanging clothes, pressing its face into Ryan's shirts. Its blond curls shone softly in the darkness.

I raced over to Ryan and picked him up out of bed. "We're getting out of here," I said, charging out of the room and towards the stairs.

It wasn't a possessed doll. Those don't exist. Someone had *put* the doll there—which meant someone was *in our house. Mark—it could be Mark. Some sort of sick, twisted way to get back at me for getting the house in the settlement.*

Did he still have the keys?

I raced down the stairs, Ryan bobbing with each step. When I got to the landing, I glanced back.

Nonononono.

The doll was at the top of the stairs, now. Face pressed into the wall.

I raced to the front door. Grabbed the doorknob, yanked it open. Glanced back.

The doll was on the landing. *And was that a shadow next to it? Someone... someone standing there?*

I ran across the front yard, towards the neighbor's house. I pounded on the door, crying. "Let me in! Someone broke into our house! *Please!*"

As I took a final glance at our house, I saw the doll leaned against the oak tree in our front yard.

The police didn't find anything. No doll, no evidence of a break-in. With nothing to go on, they left, telling me they'd call if they got in touch with Mark.

Ryan and I are staying at a friend's house for a few days, while we get our bearings and try to figure out what's going on here.

But I'm worried. Because last night, when I went to check on Ryan to see if he was asleep yet, I found an empty bed.

Ryan was standing in the corner of the room.

Leaning against the wall.

Hands over his face.

"What are you doing?" I whispered, tugging at his arm. "Go back to bed. Now."

He turned towards me, hands still pressed against his eyes.

"He isn't in time out, Mommy," he said.

I stopped in my tracks. "... What?"

"He's playing hide and seek," he continued. "Now he's hiding... and it's my turn to seek."

HAS ANYONE SEEN THE "UPSIDE-DOWN WOMAN"?

I don't believe in the supernatural. Never have, never will. But everything the last few days has me questioning *everything*. I haven't slept, I haven't eaten, I haven't left my house. Yet I fear she will get me anyway.

Let me start at the beginning.

I was driving home from a friend's party three days ago. I'd stayed late, and it was already dark out. And then something caught my eye.

On the third floor of an old Victorian house, the light was on. In the window, I saw a shape.

The shape of a woman hanging upside-down.

It was as if her feet were somehow tied to the ceiling, and she was hanging upside-down in mid-air. Her arms somehow hung naturally at her sides, defying gravity. But her hair hung straight down from her head, ending in little wispy threads.

No detail—just a silhouette.

As soon as I recognized it, I was already passed the house. So I turned around and drove past it again. This time, I only saw some rumpled curtains with tassels and a lamp in the window.

Which, maybe if you squinted real hard, could look like a woman hanging upside-down?

I shook my head and kept driving home. I'd had a lot of "pareidolia jump scares" like this. Pareidolia is our brain's tendency to see faces and shapes in randomness—like how we see clouds that look like animals, or knots of wood that look like faces.

Sometimes, I think I have an overactive sense of pareidolia. For example—years ago, when I got bangs cut for the first time, I started seeing shadow people. It took me an embarrassingly long time to realize the "shadow people" was hair falling into my eyes, that my brain was interpreting as some sort of demon or spirit.

So I didn't give the upside-down woman much thought.

Until I saw her again.

I was on the subway into work. Lights caught my eye, out the window, as another subway passed us in the opposite direction. I looked up—

And there she was.

The silhouette of a woman, hanging upside-down, in the passing subway car. Pressed against the window, blurred by the speed of the train.

I only saw her for a split-second—and then she was gone, as the train rattled past us.

What the fuck?

I must've just seen, like... a black jacket draped over a seat, or something, right? My heart began to pound.

I stared out the window for the rest of my commute. But all the other passing subways were fine, filled with commuters staring at their phones. When I got out at the station, my legs were so weak, I thought I might collapse. But I forced myself to work.

I didn't see anything strange on the way back from work, either. When I got home, I tried to distract myself, binging the nastiest stuff on HBO and plowing through an entire bag of chips.

Then, I finally went to sleep.

Only to wake up with a start at 3:03 AM.

I was covered in a film of cold sweat. My heart was pounding, but I couldn't remember any dream. Usually when I woke up like this, the vestiges of some nightmare were still in my head. This time, there was nothing.

I rolled over, pulling the covers up to my chin, and closed my eyes.

Wait.

There was something in the darkness of my room that didn't look quite right.

I opened my eyes and looked around the room, my heart hammering.

The dark shapes of my nightstand, my bookshelves, came into focus. Everything was where it should be...

Except for the light.

It was too dark in here.

I rolled back over, towards my window, and realized that the usual annoying light from the streetlamp below was not shining through the curtains.

I got out of bed, slowly, and made my way to the window.

I pulled back the curtains.

My knees buckled underneath me.

She was hanging from the roof.

Her feet were tied to the awning of the roof, right in front of my window. Her arms hung loosely from her shoulders. Her hair hung straight down, waving gently in the breeze.

Actually, *her entire body* was waving gently in the breeze.

I grabbed the curtains and pulled them shut. I ran over to the light. Then I tip-toed back to the window and peeked out a tiny slit between the curtains.

No.

She was gone.

I saw the streetlamp. The night sky, dotted with stars.

The next morning, I tried to tell myself it was a dream. I'd had a few weird moments in my life, in the twilight between dreaming and wake. Sleep is a weird, hallucinogenic continuum, and who was to say I hadn't imagined the woman out my window?

Deep down, I knew that wasn't true.

But it was a pretty little lie.

I made my way to work shaken. I didn't look up at passing subway cars. I drank about three cups of coffee. Jeff, ever the charmer, told me I looked super tired, and Tina asked me if I was sick. I didn't tell them what happened. They wouldn't believe me.

When I got home, I started searching online for what I'd seen.

I found myself scouring urban legend forums, and even old posts here on NoSleep—the kinds of places I only visited briefly when I saw the shadow people, or when I was looking for a laugh. Now, I wasn't laughing. I was desperately searching for an answer to whatever *this* was.

And then, finally, I found it.

Someone claimed their friend had seen the Upside-Down Woman, and had died four days later.

Stay away from windows, they warned. *It can only manifest in windows.*

They also remarked that their friend had at first

seen the woman through two layers of glass—like through a car window, into the window of a home—and then, later, through only one window. Like it was getting closer.

Some sciencey person had replied, asking all kinds of ridiculous questions, like if plastic counts, or any transparent material, and they replied:

There has to be a pane of glass, or glass-like material, in front of the person.

They did not explain "glass-like" any further.

There was no way to avoid windows. Unless I lived in the basement. So I moved food, water, and clothing down there while half-closing my eyes. I told my boss I was sick. *("Oh yeah, Tina told me you looked sick. Hope it's not COVID.")* It took me a long time, but then I was settled in. For how long, I didn't know. I didn't know if it was even possible to wait out the Upside-Down Woman.

And I didn't even know if I actually believed in her existence, in the first place.

That was about to change.

I decided to get some reading done to get my mind off things. I grabbed my book and, without thinking, grabbed my reading glasses.

As soon as I put them on, I screamed.

She was hanging from the basement ceiling.

Hanging in the corner. A void of darkness, hair nearly trailing to the floor.

And then, this time, *she moved.*

In jerky, incredibly fast motions, she broke free from the ceiling and scrambled towards me. I ripped the glasses off my face—but not before pain exploded in my arm.

When I looked down, there were four deep scratch marks on my forearm, dripping blood.

That leaves me here. I am sitting in my basement, away from all windows and glass, on the third day. According to the guy on the internet, his friend was killed the fourth day. I don't know what will happen after four days. If that means I've waited her out, and she'll move onto another target—or if she'll kill me anyway, glass or not.

If you don't hear from me in twenty-four hours, assume the worst.

I WORK AT A NURSING HOME FOR MONSTERS

From the outside, Shady Glen looks like any other nursing home. The lawn is perfectly manicured, the flowerbeds are in bloom, and the windows are as shiny as a mirror. If you drive by on a warm, sunny afternoon, you'll see them out there—elderly folks, walking with canes or walkers, nurses by their sides.

No one would ever guess the horrors inside.

When I first started working at Shady Glen, I was excited. I chose my career path as a geriatric nurse because I wanted to help people. Starting at a new facility always meant meeting new people, having more opportunities to make new friends and have a positive impact on someone's life. I'd already met so many wonderful people at the last nursing home I worked at, and I hoped this would be the same.

Sadly, those hopes were immediately dashed.

Generally speaking, nursing home folks are friendly. Sure, you'll get a few grumps in the bunch, but most of them *want* to talk. I've been kept way over my shift many times by someone who just *had* to finish telling me a story from their youth, or asked me to play *another* game of checkers. Don't get me wrong—I loved staying a little late to spend time with them! That's the reason I'm here—to make a difference.

But *no one* at Shady Glen wanted to talk to me.

I spent my break in the game room, and no one approached me. No little old lady with photos of her grandkids. No older guy ready to regale me with stories of his youth. They completely ignored me.

And yet... they didn't *completely* ignore me. I could see them watching me, in my peripheral vision.

There was an old lady with cotton-candy white hair in the corner, reading a book. She was just *staring* at me—until I looked at her. Then she lifted the book and pretended like she'd been reading all along. Two men were playing chess by the window, but they hadn't made a move in twenty minutes. Because they were too busy watching me.

And as I got up and walked to the trash, I saw *several* heads turning in unison, tracking my movement.

Except one.

Sitting behind the men playing chess, facing the window, was a woman. She didn't bother watching me like the others; she just stared out the window, slowly rocking back and forth in her chair.

There was one problem.

She wasn't old.

She looked somewhere in her 30s or early 40s, with long, black hair that didn't even have a single strand of gray. Her skin was pale, to the point of looking sickly, like she'd never seen the sun.

Maybe she's visiting? I thought. But it was 10 AM, and visiting hours started at noon. And she wasn't an employee—she wasn't wearing nurses' scrubs or a nametag.

I picked up my things and decided to take the rest of my break somewhere else. I felt all of their eyes on me, tracking my movement, as I walked out into the hallway.

Maybe they're just wary of new people, I thought.

Maybe they're bored and wondering who this random new guy is.

But the way all of them stared at me sent a chill down my spine. It wasn't a few nosey Nancys peering at me over a book; it was *everyone* in the room. Like they could all communicate telepathically, and were alerting each other to my presence, or something.

Except for the one weirdly young woman. She didn't seem to acknowledge my presence at all.

I wasn't sure if that was comforting, or not.

I finally found myself back in the staff break room, where a few other people were taking their break. I decided to ask some questions, to figure out what the deal was here.

"The people here aren't very talkative, are they?" I joked.

One of the guys—a physical therapist, I think—looked up at me. "What d'you mean?"

"Well, at the other places I've worked at, the seniors are really friendly. Like, dying to tell me their entire life story. But here... they're kind of quiet."

"Oh, yeah. They're all pretty private," he replied.

"And what about that one woman? The one with the black hair and the really pale skin? Is she actually a patient here? She looks way too young."

"Oh, that's Elena. Yeah, she's a patient."

"How old is she?"

He forced a smile. "She's a lot older than she looks."

"Wow. I guess she really takes sunscreen seriously," I joked. "She doesn't look a day over 40."

He didn't reply. The other people there—two women in nursing scrubs—kind of side-eyed each other. "Sorry, I gotta go," he said suddenly.

Then he walked out, the nurses following him.

Even though we still had ten minutes of break left.

I chewed my lip. So far, I wasn't making the friendships I'd imagined. Not with the seniors, *or* the staff. Which was very different than what I was used to. I'm not the most popular person, but I'm very outgoing, and usually making friends is a piece of cake.

Not here.

I cleared my trash and pulled out my phone, checking the schedule. My next patient was in room 40C. I headed down the beige hallway, glancing at the rows and rows of doors that seemed to extend forever.

When I got in front of her door, I pulled up her chart on the iPad they'd given me.

That's when I noticed something strange.

Her chart had a note scrawled across the top of it, even above her name. It read: *do not make eye contact with patient.*

That's weird, I thought. Maybe she was antisocial, or agoraphobic? I paged through her chart on the iPad, looking for details of her mental state. But there were none, other than a note about her memory starting to deteriorate.

Whatever the case, I'd honor her wishes. Even if it made my extroverted self die a little bit inside.

When I pushed the door open, she was sitting on the bed. Long gray hair fell halfway over her face. She wore a plain white dressing gown, though it appeared stained and tattered. My eyes instinctually shot towards her face—then I stopped myself and stared at the floor. "Hi, I'm Jeff," I said. "I'll be your nurse today."

She didn't respond.

"Is there anything I can get for you?" I asked. "Or can I start taking your vitals now?"

She didn't say anything, but in my peripheral vision, I saw her nod. I took that as the go ahead to start.

I pulled the metal chair towards her and sat down. "This is going to pinch a little bit, okay?" I said, wrapping the blood pressure cuff around her upper arm. I kept my eyes on the dial as it climbed, avoiding all eye contact. I felt incredibly awkward, but respecting her wishes was more important than anything.

"Just going to look in your ear now," I told her as I pulled out my otoscope. I kept my eyes on trained on her ear. In the corner of my eye, I could see her eyes peeking out from under strands of gray hair, blurred and out-of-focus.

I pulled out a tongue depressor. "Now, I'm just going to have to take a look at your throat..."

She opened her mouth and I pressed the wooden stick down. But from this angle, her eyes were just barely out of focus. And I could see something looked... off... about them. They looked like they were too big for her face, or too dark, or something. Of course, I couldn't really tell because I wasn't looking directly at her eyes, but... something didn't look right.

Maybe she had an eye appointment earlier today, and had her pupils dilated? That was the only possible explanation I could think of. Although, it wasn't just her pupils that looked bigger—it was also her irises, and her actual eyes themselves. Like she was using some weird Instagram filter to make everything about her eyes... bigger.

It was weird.

As much as I felt an instinctual tug to make eye contact, to see what was actually wrong with her eyes, I managed to avoid it. When I was done, I packed up my things, told her goodbye, and made my way to the next patient.

You did a great job, I told myself, as I made my way to room 37A. *You respected her boundaries, and I bet she really appreciated that.*

Maybe this first day isn't going to be so awful, after all.

My enthusiasm was quickly deflated by the next patient.

The man in room 37A was named Gerald. He was 86, according to the chart, but he looked like he could be a hundred. His body had shrunken in on itself, all folds and wrinkles. His tufts of white hair stood straight up, as if compensating for his loss in height. And he was friendlier than the others—as soon as I came in, he smiled at me.

"Hello. Are you my new nurse?"

I nodded and introduced myself. And just like that, I was back in the game. Gerald was easy to talk to—he asked me how long I'd been a nurse, if I liked it here. All the while, smiling and telling me he was so happy to have me here.

"My last nurse was so grumpy," he said, rolling his eyes. "But you seem like a fun one."

"Thanks," I replied. I wrapped the blood pressure cuff around his arm, and it began to inflate. "So, Gerald, where did you grow up?"

And just like that, the vibe we had going was gone.

His smile disappeared. He broke eye contact and looked vacantly at the wall. "A great distance away from here," he finally muttered.

I took the hint and didn't ask any questions. But after a minute, he started talking again. He looked up, milky gray eyes boring into mine. "I come from a place where demons roam," he muttered, his voice low and gravelly. "A place where the shadows don't need light. A place of eternal darkness."

A chill went down my spine.

To be fair, I've worked with many patients who had dementia or mental conditions, and this was far from the most horrific thing I'd heard. One man I'd worked with suffered from paranoia; every day, he'd recount the death threats he received, in painstaking detail. He was convinced people wanted him dead, in extremely violent ways, because he worked for a top-secret government agency. There was a woman, too, who always told me about the skinny woman who hid under her bed. After strict observation, we realized she was confusing some storage boxes for a human being.

It's hard being this old. When your mind starts to deteriorate, and you start blurring the lines between reality and fiction. And there's a fine line dealing with people in this state. You don't want to encourage their delusions, but you also want to make sure they feel heard.

"You must be happier here," I said.

He paused for a moment. "I'm happier here," he finally replied.

"That's great," I replied with a smile.

I finished taking his vitals, grabbed the iPad, and started back into the hallway. As I flipped through the documents, however, I noticed there was no note of dementia or any other mental condition. In fact, someone had checked "GOOD" under his mental state.

"Jeff," a voice called out behind me.

I turned. The old man had followed me out in the hallway. He was standing several yards behind me, perfectly still.

"Do you need something?" I called.

He shook his head. "They roam here, too. The demons. They're just not as loud."

I nodded and gave him a wave.

Then I added a note to his chart. Under mental conditions, I wrote, *talks about demons.*

Who was next? Someone on the second floor, by the name of Mary Gonzalez. I took the elevator and walked down the hallway. She'd be at the end, in room 29B.

It wasn't just the people who were a little off. There was something about the beige hallways, the endless doors with little square windows in them, the slightly-distorted music repeating on loop. Seriously, it sounded like a cassette player on low battery, slowing everything down, making each note a half-pitch lower.

I shuddered.

Maybe I'll send out more applications.

I didn't like it here by any stretch of the word. The stares, the weird interactions, my standoffish coworkers... there was a weird feeling to this place.

And as I walked down the hallway, I saw something even weirder.

One of the doors had a padlock on it.

I stopped and backed up. 26C. The number was faded, and the window was completely dark. *Maybe it's empty? Why lock it, then?*

I stared down at the padlock. That certainly wasn't legal. Unless the patient was a risk to others

—but even then, they should've been transferred to a hospital or something. They shouldn't be kept here, behind a locked door.

I leaned in towards the window. Totally dark. None of the hallway light even began to penetrate the darkness within.

What the hell?

I cupped my hands against the window, peering in.

And then it happened.

On the other side of the glass—an eye blinked open.

I yelped and leapt back. My ankle twisted—my feet slipped underneath me—and I fell, hard, onto the linoleum floor. Pain shot up my arms, my knees.

I scrambled up.

Above me, there was something moving in the window. A mass of black hair, parted slightly to reveal an eye. Now, I realized, the lights in the room were on. The window had only been dark because *she'd* been pressed against the window.

Watching me.

And I recognized her. Pale skin. Thick black hair. Far too young to be here...

It was the woman I'd seen earlier.

I scrambled up and ran down the hallway. I didn't stop until I'd reached 29B. Before I entered, I took a second to get a hold of myself. Deep breath in, deep breath out. My hands were shaking. My legs felt weak and wobbly underneath me.

Maybe she just has a mental condition, and needs to be housed here for a little while, I thought.

It's just a woman. Not a monster.

So she was staring at you from the window. So what? She wasn't screaming or threatening you.

But then, why the padlock?

I forced myself to take another deep breath in. And another. I didn't open the door until I felt like I was completely relaxed. *Give them your best,* I told myself, like I had many times before.

I swung the door open.

Mary sat in front of the window, looking down at the courtyard below. She was humming softly to herself—a tune I didn't recognize. However, from my high school music training, I could tell it was in minor key.

"How are you doing today, Mary?" I asked.

She didn't answer. Didn't turn around to look at me. Just continued humming the same four notes, over and over.

"Mary?"

More humming.

I pulled out the iPad and flipped through her chart. It was then that I noticed the note: *patient is nonverbal.* Okay, that made sense. No creepy weirdness here—just a nonverbal patient. I pulled a chair up and sat down next to her, narrating what I was doing so that I wouldn't startle or scare her.

"I'm going to put the blood pressure cuff on you now, okay?"

"Just going to look in your ear…"

I tugged at her ear and put the otoscope in, looking around for any signs of inflammation or infection.

But as I did, my heart stopped.

There was shadow, nestled next to her eardrum. As soon as the light hit it, it skittered out of sight.

What the hell?

I tugged on her ear, readjusted the otoscope. No —there was nothing there. No shadow. Her ear was totally fine.

I put the scope down and rubbed my eyes. *The stress is getting to you,* I told myself. I took another deep breath in, deep breath out. *It was just a shadow that moved when I moved the scope. Nothing more.*

"Your ears look great, Mary," I said. But my voice didn't have that same chipper tone.

I finished the exam. Mary continued to hum to herself. The same four notes, over and over—except she was humming them faster, now. I packed up my stuff, took another deep breath, and walked out into the hallway.

I closed my eyes as I passed room 26C.

I took the elevator down to floor 1. I took my lunch break alone. I didn't want to talk to anyone anymore. I was just going to slog through this day, and send out job applications tonight. Hopefully I'd find something else within a week or two. Maybe a month. *I can't survive a month in this place,* I thought, as I finished my turkey sandwich.

It's just too weird.

Surprisingly, however, the afternoon went smoothly. No weird demon-talk, no creepy humming... just regular old people. They didn't say much, but that was okay with me. As late afternoon crept into evening, the staff thinned out, and most of the residents returned to their rooms. At 7:45 I began packing up, more than ready to hand the reins over to the night shift.

But of course, it wasn't that easy.

My boss poked his head in and asked if I could check in with one more patient, as the night shift nurse was running late. Like an idiot, I agreed.

I was already on the second floor when I realized it was room 26C.

The woman who looked far too young to be here.

I wanted to turn around and run. But I needed this job, even if it was only for the next few weeks. And besides—they wouldn't keep someone violent here. That would be illegal. Sure, the padlock was there, but it didn't change the law. Maybe the padlock was for her own safety—to keep her from running away.

Just fifteen minutes with her, I told myself. *Then you get to go home.*

I pulled out the iPad and paged through her chart.

But most of it was blank.

Her name was filled in. Elena, with a long last name that sounded Polish or Czech from the number of consonants. But there was just a dash for her birthdate. *Did they not know her age?* And there was nothing under the current medications section. No chronic illnesses, either. No diabetes, no arthritis, not even hearing loss.

If she truly didn't have any of these things, why was she here?

Or did someone give me an incomplete chart?

Better yet... if this chart was incomplete, maybe it would give me an excuse to not do the exam today and just go home. If she had some underlying medical condition I wasn't aware of, it could be a liability.

I walked down the hallway and, after a second, found one of the doctors on staff. "Hey, uh, I think this chart for Elena is incomplete," I told him.

"No, that's her chart," he replied, as he gave it a quick once-over.

"But nothing's filled in. Not even her birthdate."

"We don't know her birthdate."

I stared at him. "You don't *know* her birthdate?"

He shook his head.

"What about approximate age, then? Or, medical conditions? The entire thing's just blank."

The doctor stared back at me. "I assure you, the chart is accurate," he replied, in a strangely firm tone.

Then he turned on his heel and walked away.

My stomach twisted again. Something deep inside me, saying *this isn't right. Something is wrong here.* A little voice in the back of my head, telling me to leave, to get out.

Nothing about this felt right.

I walked back to Elena's room. Someone had already undone the padlock for me. I took a deep breath and pushed the door open; it squeaked loudly on its hinges.

Elena was sitting next to the window, facing away from me. Black hair cascaded down the back of her chair, and her pale arms hung limply at her sides.

"Hi, I'm Jeff," I called from the doorway, my heart pounding. "I'll... I'll be taking your vitals this evening."

She didn't reply.

That was fine by me. I'd rather her ignore me than the alternative.

I pulled up a chair next to her and unfolded the blood pressure cuff. The Velcro zipped loudly in the silent room. "I'm going to take your blood pressure," I told her.

No response.

I wrapped it around her upper arm. The rhythmic *thu-wump* of the cuff inflating filled the silence. Still, she wouldn't turn to look at me, or acknowledge my presence in any way. She just stared out the window, the harsh shadows making her skin appear even paler than it was before.

Thu-wump, thu-wump...

The blood pressure cuff continued to inflate. Elena continued to stare out the window, ignoring me completely. *This will all be over soon. Log the vitals and get the hell out of here.*

Except there was a problem.

I wasn't getting a blood pressure reading.

That's weird. I squinted at the dial, then reached up and pulled it off her arm. "Sorry. I think I might've messed up..."

But a second and third attempt failed. I couldn't get a reading. I swallowed, my throat dry. *Screw it,* I thought. "Elena, I'm going to take your blood pressure later. For now, I'm going to check your ears, okay?"

No response.

She still wouldn't turn towards me. Or acknowledge my presence in any way. So I glanced at her reflection in the window, to try and read her expression.

Every muscle in my body froze.

She didn't *have* a reflection.

I only saw my horrified face, staring back at me.

No. No, that's not possible. I stood up, the chair skidding out from underneath me. I stumbled towards the hallway, dropping the blood pressure cuff in the process. "I'm sorry," I muttered, scrambling to the door. "I'll come back later—"

A shuffling sound came from behind me.

I whipped around.

The woman had finally turned to look at me.

But her body was still facing the window.

She had turned her head all the way around, in a way no human could do.

I ran. I ran as fast as I could. Down the hallway, around the corner, my feet slapping against the floor. As I passed the game room, I saw a few heads turning towards me, tracking my movement.

But I didn't stop. I just kept running.

And then I heard it.

SLAP.

The woman was following me.

She was crawling along the hallway on all fours, like something possessed. Her head hung upside-down, her thick black hair dragging along the floor. Her mouth was twisted into a smile and her teeth— *her teeth*—they were pointed, all of them, into needle-thin fangs.

SLAP, SLAP, SLAP.

Her palms slapped against the linoleum as she

crawled towards me, spider-like. Her mouth frozen in that horrible grin.

I forced myself to run faster. I was almost there, almost at the elevator—

SLAPSLAPSLAP!

I glanced back. She was so fast, scuttling towards me—

Something grabbed me by the arm.

I let out a yelp. My entire body jerked. But I wasn't being pulled backwards—I was being pulled to the right. Into a room. The door slammed shut and I found myself face-to-face with another nurse.

It was one of the nurses I'd seen earlier in the break room. She looked at me with wide eyes, breathing hard.

"What's... what *is* she?" I breathed, backing away from the door.

"You can't do that," she replied, advancing towards me.

"Can't do... what?"

"I'm not going to hurt you," she said, hurriedly. "I'm trying to keep you safe. You can't run away from them like that. They smell fear."

"But—"

"Once you're here, they know you. They know your smell. They'll follow you. Anywhere in the world you go, you'll be followed. But if you stay here, and don't run, and do what you're asked, you'll be safe."

"What are you talking about?"

"They will follow you. If you run out of this building, they will follow. They don't want their secrets to leave this place. Just do your job, don't show fear, and you'll be safe."

She unlocked the door and swung it open.

"I think you have an exam to finish."

Maybe I should've listened to her. This woman who was probably looking out for my own good, looking to protect me. She did just save me, after all. But as soon as she opened that door—I shot out and ran into the elevator.

I pounded the *close doors* button as Elena skittered down the hall, as the nurse shouted after me.

The doors shut and the elevator car went down, down, down.

I raced out into the parking lot and got in my car. The engine thrummed underneath me, and I peeled out of there.

But not before taking one last glance at Shady Glen.

There was someone watching me from a second story window. Someone with thick black hair and pale skin.

I swallowed.

Then I turned onto the road and floored it.

———

I spent the evening trying to forget everything that happened. I got a voicemail from my boss, asking where I went, but I ignored it. I got a few calls from unknown numbers, and I ignored them too.

The nightmare at Shady Glen was over. I was done with that place. The patients there aren't human. They're monsters. The woman with the eyes that were too big. The man who talked about demons. The woman with the thing in her ear. And, of course, Elena. That entire building, from the patients to the endless halls to the strange, distorted music through the speakers.

The nightmare was over.

Or so I thought.

Unfortunately, I woke up with a start at 3:00 AM.

As I stirred into consciousness, I realized what woke me up was a noise. A soft *tap-tap-tap* coming from somewhere. I grabbed my phone off the night stand and stood up, trying to place the source of the noise.

it sounded like it was coming from downstairs.

I made my way to the stairs, my heart pounding. I typed in 911 on my phone, ready to press call. The tapping continued as I made my way down the stairs. *Tap-tap-tap.*

When I got to the bottom, I turned towards the kitchen—and that's when I saw it.

Someone was tapping at the sliding glass door in the kitchen.

Someone with long black hair, pale skin, and needle-like teeth.

Elena.

I immediately ducked out of sight. But as soon as I did, the tapping got faster. *Taptaptaptap.*

She had seen me.

I ran back up the stairs, my heart pounding. The nurse's warning echoed in my head. *They'll follow you. Anywhere in the world you go, you'll be followed. But if you stay here, and don't run, and do what you're asked, you'll be safe.*

I got back to my bedroom and slammed the door shut. Locked it. Pulled the dresser across it. I called 911, and they assured me they'd be here soon.

Then I got in the closet, closed the door, and waited.

For a few minutes, I didn't hear anything. Just pure silence. *Maybe she left,* I told myself. *The police will be here any minute.* I took deep breaths in and out, trying to slow my heart, trying to relax. *The police will be here any minute.*

But then the tapping resumed.

Tap, tap, tap.

Coming from my bedroom window.

My second story bedroom window.

I didn't dare look. But I could imagine her spider-like body, clinging to the side of my house.

Her long fingers, tapping against the glass. Thick black hair falling over her face. Needle-like teeth bared in a horrible grin.

Tap, tap, tap.

A minute later, I heard the sirens. And the tapping stopped. I heard a scuttling sound as she made her way down the house; and then there was nothing. The sirens grew louder, and my heart slowed, knowing I was safe.

Except I wasn't safe. I never would be, according to the nurse.

Unless I came back.

So that morning, after zero hours of sleep and three cups of coffee, I drove to Shady Glen. I passed the manicured lawns, the elderly sitting on benches and enjoying the warm, sunny morning. I parked and walked through the front doors, down the endless beige hallways, listening to the slowed music playing through the speakers. I picked up the iPad and checked my first assignment.

Then I took the elevator up to the fourth floor, repeating the same three words over and over again in my head.

Don't show fear.

THERE'S SOMETHING WRONG WITH MY HUSBAND'S PAINTINGS

My husband is a painter.

Well... that's a stretch. He does very modern, Jackson Pollock-style art. I've seen him in the studio, and he's not so much *painting* as he is flinging paint at the canvas with his bare hands.

Strangely, though, people pay real money for his work. His most recent one, gray and blue splatters on a gray canvas entitled *Ocean Dawn,* fetched us a cool $3,000. He makes a full salary off his work, and then some.

I don't get it. Maybe the people who buy his work are smarter or more "cultured" than me. They all fit a very specific type—well-dressed men with distinguished salt-and-pepper hair, petite blonde wives that look like they've never eaten a slice of cake in their lives. Money to burn, put on the dog types.

Although, if it's a choice between one of my husband's paintings and a Louis Vuitton purse... well, his paintings are (marginally) less ugly than those purses. Man, what is it with rich people and ugly stuff?

Anyway. I'm getting off on a tangent here. The reason why I'm writing this is because my husband has been away for the past two weeks visiting family. While he's been gone, I've been running the business by myself, and I've noticed some... *odd*... things.

His studio is a really nice space downtown. Large and full of light. Filled ceiling to floor with his paintings. And even though they're individually ugly, there's something sort of beautiful about them being all together. The different colors and splattering types all match and coordinate with each other—it's obvious they're all done by the same artist.

Maybe that's why he makes money off them. They have a distinct style. You can point to one and say, with certainty, **that's** *a Theodore Waters painting. The thick globs of paint, the colors that don't really go with each other—that's a Waters right there.*

I could put on a smock and throw paint at a canvas while listening to Gregorian chants, too, but I wouldn't be able to produce paintings that consistently resembled each other in style.

The first few days went well. We had a minor

hiccup—I almost gave the woman buying *Evening Tranquility* the wrong painting (they looked identical to me!). But I was enjoying it. After work, I'd head to the studio for a few hours and binge dramas on Hulu, waiting for the next client to come by.

Things took a turn for the worse, however, on Wednesday night.

My iPad ran out of battery twenty minutes before the last client was supposed to show up. So I just... sat there, staring at the paintings. I got up and rearranged them a little. I pulled out the piece that was supposed to be sold tonight—*Midnight Dream*.

It was one of the less ugly ones, if only for its color scheme. Black canvas, or possibly navy blue, splattered with purple, mauve, indigo, and white. And just a few dots of ocean blue, drizzling across the front. I leaned it against the other paintings and sat back at the desk, taking off my glasses and rubbing my eyes. Damn allergies.

When I looked back up, however, I froze.

With my glasses off, *Midnight Dream* was now blurry. And with all the random splatters blurred now, I could see a clear shape. How there were less splatters, more darkness, in the center of the canvas.

That looked exactly like the silhouette of a person.

A person leaned over the viewer, staring down at them.

What the...

I put my glasses back on. But with all the clear dots and drizzles and specks, I could only barely make out the image.

Was *that* why people were buying Theodore's paintings?

Because there was a second, hidden image?

It didn't make sense, though. I'd *seen* Theodore making some of these paintings. He was randomly flinging paint on a canvas, listening to those calming Gregorian chants or whatever they were. There was no way he could *plan* where the paint fell, to create a second image.

Unless he was somehow going back and painting over some of the paint splatters later. Though I didn't see any brush strokes to imply that.

I got up and pulled out another one of Theodore's paintings. Entitled *Pink Marble*—splatters of pink and red and white. I leaned it against *Midnight Dream,* stepped back, and took off my glasses.

It was a hand.

A hand covered in splatters of blood.

My stomach did a little flip. I felt nauseous. *It's just art,* I told myself. *People do extreme art all the time. What about that one where that giant guy is eating a man? That's like, in an art museum and everything, right?*

Nothing wrong with painting a bloody hand.

Nothing wrong with painting a shadow person glaring down at you.

And maybe I was wrong. There wasn't much detail in these images, just the *suggestion* of forms. It could be pareidolia, my brain assigning familiar shapes to the paintings. Like a Rorschach test. Maybe these *were* random blobs and it was just my imagination.

I took out another painting.

This one was pretty ugly: muddy shades of brown and green around the edges, a big pink blob in the middle. *Spring Blooms* was the title.

I leaned it against *Pink Marble* and stepped back. Closed my eyes, let out a breath. Took off my glasses.

I opened my eyes.

Oh, no...

The pinkish blob, now blurred and at a distance, was clearly the shape of a woman's body. Laying on the ground. Splattered with blood.

Why would he paint this?

*And who would **buy** this?*

Who would want a painting of a dead body in their home?

I swallowed, my throat dry. I put on my glasses and slid the painting back in with the others stacked up. Was this the reason Theodore was actually making money? He was selling these paintings to sickos, that were camouflaged well enough to stay hung up through dinner parties and visits from the in-laws?

I texted the client who was supposed to pick up *Midnight Dream* and told them I wasn't feeling well. Then I drove home, stomach twisting, and locked myself inside.

But I didn't exactly feel safe in the house, either. Because Theodore had a few of his own paintings hanging on our walls. I realized now, as I viewed them from a distance, that the painting in our living room depicted a close-up of a woman's face—but something black was oozing out of her mouth. *Vomit? A spider?* Not enough detail to tell. And the huge one in our bedroom, hanging above our bed, looked like two lovers embracing—except they appeared dead, from the ashen-gray tint of their bodies.

This was sick.

And it didn't even make sense. I remembered when Theodore painted this one, the one of the lovers. I had watched him for more than an hour. He was just flinging paint randomly as he listened to the weird chanting music he always played. Yet the blobby shapes clearly suggested two people embracing.

I decided to sleep in the guest room that night.

But before I did, I made the mistake of walking into Theodore's home studio.

I'd left the lights on, somehow, so I stepped into

the studio, my heart pounding. It was a lot more cramped than the one downtown—only about 100 square feet, with a huge stack of paintings in the corner.

As I reached for the light switch, I noticed the unfinished piece on the easel.

I'd seen it several times over the last few weeks. But now, I saw it differently. I took off my glasses and took a few steps back, out into the darkened foyer.

It was a woman, lying on a dark wooden floor, splattered in blood.

Except that woman... was *me*.

Of course I couldn't be sure. There wasn't enough detail. But from the colors, that looked like *my* favorite gray sweater, *my* hair splayed out on the floor.

I backed away.

Then I ran out of the house.

I drove all night until I got to a friend's place. That's where I am now. Theodore has tried to call me, but I've let all his calls go to voicemail.

Every time I close my eyes, I see the painting.

The splatters of paint that look just like my dead body.

THERE ARE STRANGE FOOTPRINTS IN THE SNOW

I found them on my back porch.

Imprints in the snow of two bare feet—pointing in opposite directions.

The left foot was pointed at the house, but the right foot was pointed at the treeline. Like someone had been standing at my back door, but one of their feet had been severed and stuck on backwards.

They continued like that in a sinuous line that disappeared into the woods.

I tried the position myself, tried to twist one foot all the way around. It wouldn't go. The best I could do was a sort of L-shape, with one foot vertical, one horizontal.

Even normal footprints would be terrifying, as the nearest neighbor was a tenth-mile away. But barefoot, in the snow? Barefoot, with one foot *backwards?*

I decided to get the hell out of dodge. I made an impromptu visit to a friend, working remotely from her guest bedroom. The next morning, however, I found footprints in the icy snow at *her* back door.

One pointed forward, one pointed back.

I sat down and thought. *Could it be an ex? Brandon didn't take our breakup well, not at all.* He was a closeminded, selfish fool, but I'd still felt bad for the way he'd sobbed on the other end of the line when I'd broken it off.

Or, someone at work, maybe? Jimmy?

Or some weird prank?

Nothing made sense.

I visited my mom. My dad. I even visited my *stepsister,* who I hate. Each time, I found the same prints at her back door.

This thing, whatever it was, followed me everywhere.

So I finally went back at the cabin, two weeks after the initial sighting, after police had searched the place several times over. This time, I set up security cameras everywhere. Eight in total, all around my property.

I would catch this fucker, no matter what.

The next morning, I reviewed the footage.

In the grainy, black-and-white footage, I saw a shape emerge from the tree-line. It approached, coming into focus.

Something was horribly wrong with its face.

Half of it was shadowy and dark, while the other half was pale. And the way it walked... it looked horribly grotesque, with one knee bent the correct way, the other bent backwards.

My heart stopped as it stepped fully into the light.

It was a man. A man who appeared to be cut in half, straight down the middle, and sewn back together. Half of him facing the wrong way.

And I remembered, with horrible clarity, what I'd said to Brandon during our last phone call.

That's your problem, I'd told him. *That's always been your problem.*

You only see things from one perspective.

You have to be able to see things from two.

As I watched the man amble towards my house, one wide eye roving over the back door, the other pointed towards the forest, I realized he'd done exactly what I'd asked.

AI KEEPS TAGGING MY DEAD FRIEND IN PHOTOS

I use a photo storage service. It's like Google or Apple Photos, with some AI-powered features and facial recognition. One of the things it does is tag people that it recognizes across multiple photos.

It keeps tagging my friend, Addie Hemsworth.

There's just one problem—she's been dead for a year.

She passed our sophomore year. I won't go into details because I don't want to doxx myself here. Addie Hemsworth is not her real name. But her death made national news.

(Of course it did—it was the homicide of a white, female college student. The racist mainstream media eats those cases up like crack.)

Anyway, the whole tagging thing started a week ago. I was scrolling through photos from Mike's birthday party, when I noticed the app was tagging Addie.

The circled area was right over my shoulder. Like Addie was standing right behind me. Except, of course, she wasn't.

I zoomed in on the darkness and turned the brightness up on my phone, but I couldn't see anything; just mashed pixels and blobby darkness.

I assumed it was just a glitch, although the app had never tagged anyone wrong before.

But then it happened *again*.

I took a selfie of myself because I'd done my hair for the frat party later. And the app suggested the same thing. It circled a little space behind me, with the name *Addie*.

As if she were standing behind my bed.

This time, however, the circle was several feet off the ground. Even if she were alive, even if she were standing behind me—she wouldn't be anywhere that high. A chill ran down my spine.

I decided I needed to get out. I ran out of the dorm and walked randomly up-campus, towards the language art lecture halls, all held in enormous gothic stone buildings. The first leaves were beginning to turn orange, like the sunlight was singeing just the edges of campus. A couple laughed as they passed me. A bird squawked somewhere. I kept walking, foot over foot.

I found myself standing at the entrance of Addie's dorm. Denton hall. 12B. I looked up at the window. It was closed. 12B had stayed empty this year, out of respect for Addie.

I lifted my phone—

And took a photo.

I waited for the photo to auto-sync with the photo storage app, and then—holding my breath—I took a peek.

Nothing.

It didn't say Addie was in the photo.

I let out the breath I'd been holding and started walking back towards my dorm. Halfway back, when I came across a tree half-way orange, in the throes of autumn unlike the others, I lifted my phone and snapped a photo without even thinking about it.

Later that evening, I realized the app said Addie was there.

The circle was on the grass, as if she were lying on the ground.

...Dead?

The most horrible image flashed through my head—of Addie sprawled out on the ground, covered in gashes. Blood pooling on the ground, seeping through the grass. Sightless eyes turned towards me, mouth hanging open.

17 stab wounds, they said.

I shut my eyes and forced the image out of my

head. Then I took a screenshot and sent it to our group chat. *Lol my phone thinks addie is in this photo,* I wrote, trying to pass it off as a joke, as some kind of fucked-up defense mechanism.

Three dots appeared. And then a text from Priyanka:

I thought it was only me.

She sent a screenshot of her iPhone photo app. The most recent photo of Addie, the app claimed, was a photo of Priyanka and Greg standing under one of the gothic archways on campus. No one else was in the photo.

My throat went dry.

It could be a glitch once, maybe twice, on my phone. But if it was happening to my friends' phones, too...

Before I could reply, another text came in.

From Adam.

It's happening to me too.

I stared at my phone, feeling chills.

What the fuck?

I got up and walked across the hallway to the girls' bathroom, every bit of my body shaking. I went to the sink and stared at my reflection.

Deep bags lay under my eyes. My dark hair was tangled and uncombed. I didn't remember looking this bad earlier. I shut my eyes tight and shook my head, trying to shake the anxiety out of me.

Then I opened my eyes.

All the blood drained out of my face.

There were two feet poking out from under one of the stall doors. Wearing mint green flip-flops.

Her flip-flops.

The polish on her bare toes was chipped. Dark liquid pooled under her flip-flops. It slowly crept over the grout between the tiles, towards the floor drain, towards *me*.

No no no.

I whipped around.

Nothing was there.

I burst back into the dorm room, my heart hammering. I broke out in sobs, holding myself, shaking. This was the one time I hated not having roommates, hated that I was so introverted I made sure to get a single.

No one to hear me.

When I'd recovered slightly, I picked up my phone to text the group. The floor fell out under me when I saw the notification from the photos app.

Addie Hemsworth was tagged *in every single one* of my photos.

The phone fell out of my hands and clattered to the floor.

I closed my eyes and cried harder, unable to move. When I finally opened them, through my blurry tears, I noticed something different.

There were two shiny scars slicing up my arms.

I tore off my clothes. There were more. I counted every single one—but I already knew how many there would be.

Seventeen.

I'M THE CUSTODIAN FOR AN ELEMENTARY SCHOOL

I started working as a custodian at Shady Oaks Elementary two days ago. I expected it to be like all the other custodial jobs I'd worked—boring and a bit gross, but at least quiet and safe.

Unfortunately, my night at Shady Oaks was anything but safe.

My hours were in the evening, from eight PM to two AM, when the students had long gone home and were tucked safely in their beds. I was supposed to thoroughly clean the two bathrooms on the first floor, clean all the classrooms, and take out the garbage.

I was actually a bit excited for this job. Shady Oaks was in a nice part of town. It was set far back from the main road, among a grove of oak trees. It was also the first private school that I'd ever worked for, which would be interesting.

As soon as I pulled into the parking lot, I was impressed. The main entrance was flanked with decorative stone pillars, and a bronze statue of a little girl reading on a bench. I stopped to admire a large photo that hung in the entryway: several dozen students standing next to their teachers in old-timey clothing, smiling at the camera. The caption underneath read *first year of classes, 1957*.

I stepped into the hallway and flicked on the lights—but they didn't work. "Well, that sucks," I muttered to myself. At least there was ambient light from some of the classrooms, spilling out in bright rectangles across the shiny linoleum floor. I'd be able to find my way around without a problem.

I made my way to the main office first to get my cleaning supplies. Surprisingly, on the desk, I found a folded envelope with my name on it. Underneath, it read *from Michael Banks, Headmaster.*

I smiled. Usually, the principals and headmasters, and even the teachers, didn't really care who the custodians were. We were supposed to be invisible, neither seen nor heard, only known by our work. Like those Scottish fairy tale creatures who cleaned while everyone was asleep. It was a pretty sad reality, and dehumanizing at times, so it was nice to see that someone actually bothered to welcome me here.

I unfolded the letter and began to read.

Dear Ryan,

Thank you so much for accepting your position as custodian at Shady Oaks Elementary School! We are thrilled to have you. I am writing this letter to inform you that there are a few rules you must follow to make sure that everything gets cleaned properly and safely. The parents who send their children here expect a lot for the tuition they pay, and we want to make sure nobody is displeased.

Rule 1: Safety is of utmost importance at Shady Elms. Every afternoon, we do a full sweep of the classrooms and hallways to make sure no students have been left behind. If you ever hear a child while you're on duty, do not investigate. Even if you hear them calling for help, do not answer. Instead, enter the nearest classroom and stay inside until midnight. However, make sure you are not in Classroom Seven (see rule 2.)

Rule 2: Do not enter Classroom Seven after midnight, even if it hasn't been cleaned yet.

Rule 3: We thoroughly erase all chalkboards before we leave. If you find anything written on a chalkboard, erase it.

Rule 4: While cleaning the classrooms, put each chair upside-down on top of its desk, so that you may sweep more thoroughly. However, if any of the seats feel heavier than they should, leave them where they are.

Rule 5: If you find Locker 108 open, do not close it.

Rule 6: Clean the bathrooms thoroughly and sanitize all the countertops. We want to minimize the spread of bacteria, viruses, and other diseases. That being said, if you find a clump of hair in the bathroom sink, leave the bathroom immediately. Do not re-enter.

Rule 7: If the projector in any of the classrooms turns on, immediately leave that classroom and do not enter it for the rest of the night.

Rule 8: The school library is currently undergoing renovations. Your only job is to remove the trash in the wastebasket at the entryway of the library. Do not complete any other tasks. Spend as little time in the library as possible.

Rule 9: When cleaning the computer lab, please power down all the computers. If the computers turn on again, however, leave the room immediately. Do not look at the monitors as you leave.

Rule 10: Keep salt on you at all times. You may need it.

That's a weird list of rules, I thought. *But whatever. I'll try to follow them, I guess—don't want to get anyone mad on the first day.*

I walked over to the janitorial closet and started getting the cleaning supplies out. Before leaving the office, though, I hesitated. *Keep salt on you at all times.* It was a super weird request... but I found myself walking back into the office and searching for salt. After a bit of searching, I found some packets in a desk drawer, from some fast food place. I pocketed them and headed out.

I decided to start with the school library, since that was the easiest. I could change out a garbage bin in thirty seconds flat.

I walked down the hallway, rows of lockers extending into the darkness on either side of me. At the end of the hallway were two double doors that led to the library, if the map I'd been given was correct.

There was a plaque next to the library doors. It read: *Donated by Ephraim and Janice Smith, 1997.* For a moment, I wondered how much money they had to donate for that little piece of metal on the wall. Then I shook my head, pushed the doors open, and walked inside.

Wow. When they said the library was undergoing renovations, they meant it. There were large sheets of translucent plastic placed over all the bookshelves and the floor. A thin layer of drywall dust had settled into the wrinkles. The desk at the front of the library, where I imagined the librarian would sit, was empty.

Despite all the plastic, I couldn't pinpoint where the renovations were, exactly. I didn't see new paint on the walls, new windows, or anything like that. In fact, the library didn't have any windows, even though it was at the end of the hall, which meant it was at one of the corners of the building.

Come on, hurry up, I told myself. *The rule said stay in here as little as possible.* I glanced around and immediately found the wastebasket. I grabbed the plastic lip of the bag and pulled it out.

The trash was what I expected: candy wrappers, some papers. There was a sticky red substance smeared on one of the papers—candy or paint? I tied the bag up and then pulled out a new one, putting it into the bin.

That's when I heard a soft thump coming from one of the aisles.

"Hello?" I called out. "Anyone there?"

Nothing.

I leaned slightly, to get a full view of the aisle where I thought I'd heard the noise.

I didn't see anyone, but I did see now where the renovations were happening. There was a patch of wall at the end of that aisle that didn't match the rest. It looked like it had been freshly plastered and painted—I could see the line where new wall met old.

Why did they need to cover the entire library in plastic if they were just working on that little area?

I finished placing the new trash bag and stood up—and that's when I noticed something else. It looked like there were child's footprints in the dust on the plastic. Especially near where the wall was being repaired. Wouldn't the school block off this room from the students during the day?

I turned around and shut the door.

Then I continued down the hallway and went into the computer lab.

It was pitch dark in the room, save for a dozen little blue lights from the computers. I flicked the light switch and found myself staring at rows of computers, screens dark, with colorful mousepads featuring cartoon characters.

The computers, however, looked... old? Big, clunky monitors connected to large computers under the desks. Like the kind of computers you'd see in the early 2000s. *Doesn't a private school have enough money to buy new computers for the students?* I shook my head, scoffing. *Probably goes right into the headmaster's pocket instead.*

I swept for twenty minutes. It was monotonous work, made harder by the tangle of cords under each desk. I turned off each computer, then wiped down the desks as well, even though they didn't ask me to. There were sprinklings of crumbs everywhere, despite the clear "NO FOOD OR DRINK" sign on the door.

I was wiping down the last row of desks when I heard it.

A distinctive *whoomph* sound.

And all at once, every monitor turned on.

I turned off the computers. I know I did. I quickly averted my eyes, remembering the rules, and backed down the aisle, staring down at my feet. The rule didn't make sense, but maybe it was a test. Maybe they had security cameras, and they'd be watching my shift and making sure I followed all of them. Who knew.

I continued down the aisle, staring at the ground.

Even though I wasn't looking at the monitors, I could see the reflection of their light on the linoleum floor. And I could see... something on the monitor was *moving*. It wasn't constant, white light, but flickering and moving and changing in brightness. A high-pitched, static whine filled the room.

I stepped out into the hallway and slammed the door shut.

I wondered briefly if I should go back in and unplug all the computers—that had to be some sort of fire hazard, right? But the rules were clear. So I continued down the hallway, away from the weird computer lab.

And I bumped into an open locker.

The metal door hit me right in the face. I stepped back, face stinging, and raised my hand to close it—when I saw the number on the door.

Locker 108.

The rules had said something about that, hadn't

they? *If you find Locker 108 open, do not close it.* I sucked in a breath and removed my hand.

Then I glanced into the locker.

For a fleeting moment—I thought I saw something in the shadows of the locker. A figure, crouched in there, sitting on the bottom, knees to its chest. But I blinked and it was gone. Nothing was there. The locker was empty.

I sucked in a slow breath, trying to slow my pounding heart.

This is ridiculous. You're scaring yourself over nothing.

It was a school in the middle of nowhere, and the hallway lights didn't work. That didn't mean it was haunted or cursed or a serial killer was waiting in the shadows. I'd cleaned lots of desolate buildings before, in the dead of night. Everything from college buildings to law offices. This was just another job, another paycheck—nothing more. Yeah, the headmaster gave me a weird list of rules, but that didn't *really* mean anything... did it? It was just a test, and they were very particular about things, right?

I forced everything out of my head and started cleaning the classrooms.

I started with Classroom One. It was decorated nicely, with world maps and art all across the walls. Unfortunately, it seemed like these entitled rich kids left their classrooms far messier than their public school counterparts. There were crayons on the floor, candy wrappers, and a piece of gum stuck to one of the desks—not the bottom of the desk, but the *top*.

Gross.

I picked up the gum and began sweeping the floor, wondering if this job was going to be a lot harder than I imagined. If all the classrooms looked like this, I won't be done until dawn. I put on a podcast and began sweeping.

When I got to the front of the row, I noticed that something had been written on the chalkboard. *Was it always like that?* I thought, stepping closer.

It was in a child's handwriting, written at child-height, only a few feet off the ground. Just four words.

You don't belong here.

What's this? Some note left by a bully? That's awful, telling some kid they don't belong here, I thought. I grabbed the eraser. The message became a streaky, messy smudge.

I'd had my fair share of bullying in school. Erasing the message was a bit cathartic.

Then I went back to sweeping the floor. Even though I was only done with about half the classroom, I already had a sizable pile of garbage. Man, these kids were absolute pigs.

It took me another half hour to finish up. Then I was finally done, and moving on to Classroom Two.

This time, I noticed the writing on the chalkboard right away. One word:

Run.

It was also in a child's handwriting. In fact, it looked like the same handwriting as the previous message.

I stood there in front of the chalkboard, staring at it. One message made sense, but two? Wouldn't the teachers or someone have seen it? And why would a bully write different messages across different chalkboards?

Something didn't sit right with me. But I swallowed it down, erased the message, and started to sweep. I had a lot of work to do—at this rate I wouldn't be done until school started in the morning.

I lifted all the chairs and swept underneath them, picking up a good pile of dust, candy wrappers, hair, and even a wayward shoelace. Actually... that was weird. I leaned in closer, staring at the pile of debris.

There was, like, a *lot* of hair.

Long, black hair, curling in with all the dust and garbage.

Did someone cut their hair in here?

Between the messages on the chalkboard, and the hair, I was starting to get the impression that these teachers *really* didn't watch their students. It made sense, honestly; if some rich lady is paying twenty thousand dollars a year, she's going to be hella mad if her kid comes home crying, saying a teacher yelled at him.

I was suddenly thankful I didn't have to be here during the day. Those poor teachers.

I finished cleaning Classroom Two and headed across the dark hallway to Classroom Three. But as soon as I stepped inside, I noticed another message on the chalkboard.

This time, it was in all-caps, and the handwriting was jagged and frantic. It read:

DON'T TURN AROUND.

I froze in the doorway.

It's just some kid trying to scare people, I told myself, forcing myself to take deep breaths. *Just some kid. Just a funny prank. Nothing to see here.* I walked over to the chalkboard, picked up the eraser, and swiped it across the message. The message blurred. I swiped it back and forth, frantically, kicking up white dust. Until the message was nothing but a ghost.

Then I took a deep breath, composed myself, and began to sweep.

The rhythmic sound of the bristles against the linoleum floor calmed me. I kept my eyes down the entire time, not looking up at the doorway. It was stupid, me listening to some message left by a kid in chalk—but I couldn't help but feel like it was true. A warning.

This whole place was starting to terrify me at my core. Not to mention I was in the middle of nowhere, set back in the oak trees. Where was the nearest person, even? Someone at the liquor store in the mostly-abandoned strip mall, half a mile down the road? Someone breaking into the defunct Blockbuster again?

I was in the middle of nowhere, in a dark, creepy school. I swallowed and tried to push the fear out of my mind, focusing on my sweeping.

When I was done, I skipped over to Classroom Seven. I still had twenty minutes before midnight, and I needed to get that one done before midnight, according to the rules.

With relief, I noticed this classroom didn't have anything written on the chalkboard. I got to sweeping and putting the chairs on their desks.

This room was more colorfully decorated than the others. There were banners on the wall and a photo collage on the bulletin board. Cut-out rainbow letters read *Mrs. Thompson's Classroom.* I scratched my head. That name sounded familiar. In fact, there was something about this entire classroom that looked familiar. A fleeting but powerful sense of déjà vu. But I had never been to this school before. Today was my first day.

I continued sweeping the floor. When I got near the back of the classroom, something caught my eye. Etched onto one of the desks was a stylized S. I let out a chuckle. I remembered making those back in elementary school. It was one of those things that everybody did. In fact, I remember etching one into a desk, just like this kid had done.

I was surprised that in such a snobby rich kids' school, they hadn't immediately painted over it or something. Maybe they didn't have quite the budget I thought they did.

I continued lifting chairs and balancing them on the desks. Unlike the other rooms, these chairs were colorful. They weren't chic shades of white, blue, and green; they were bright fire-truck red, sunny yellow, lime green, ocean blue. They were definitely in worse shape than the other chairs, too, with hairline cracks and chips along their plastic structure.

I was almost done putting the chairs on their desks when I saw it.

The bulletin board of smiling children. I stopped and straightened, looking at the photo near the middle. My heart began to pound. *No, it can't be*, I told myself. *There's no way...*

The little boy in the photo looked exactly like me.

Short dark hair, pale skin, blue eyes. He was even wearing my favorite shirt back then as a kid—the shirt I wore almost every day in second grade, the one with the giant shark on it. My heart sank into my throat, and I felt lightheaded.

Mrs. Thompson. That's right, she was my second-grade teacher.

I wheeled around the room, taking in all the decorations. They were all so familiar, filling spaces in my head. I could almost hear children's voices singing the national anthem when she taught it to us. I could almost hear Billie's grating laugh, as he teased another kid. The world spun around me, and my legs felt weak.

Just a coincidence, I tried to tell myself. *Just a coincidence.*

But it couldn't be. Because I recognized the other kids on the bulletin board too. I saw Billy and his evil little grin. I saw Megan, the only girl who was nice to me. I saw nerdy little Benjamin, who I still kept in touch with, and snotty little Jessica. Faces that had eroded from my memory—just ghosts in my head—now clear as day on the board.

I didn't bother putting the rest of the chairs back. I just stumbled out of the room and back into the hallway.

When I glanced back at the window in the door, the classroom looked different. It was just another one of the generic Shady Oaks classrooms, with stylish muted colors and maps on the walls.

What's happening to me?

Did I just imagine that whole thing?

I suddenly felt too hot. The custodian uniform stuck to my skin. There's no way I'd imagined all of that, was there? I took a deep breath in and a deep breath out. I'd been having some mental health struggles lately—had I suddenly gotten much, much worse? Had something triggered a full-blown *hallucination?!*

Deep breath in, deep breath out, I told myself.

I walked down the hallway, deciding I would take a break from classrooms and start on the bathrooms.

This was going to be the worst job, but honestly, anything was better than that classroom. I got my mop and bucket and rolled them into the bathroom, the sound of the wheels echoing in the empty hallway. I dipped the mop into the soapy water, slid it across the floor, and repeated. Somehow the repetition eased some of my stress away.

Surprisingly, the bathroom was pretty clean compared to the rest of the school. I finished mopping the floor and started replacing the toilet paper. As I passed the sink, however, I saw something that made my entire body freeze.

A clump of long, dark hair, sticking to the drain.

I stared at the hair, my knees going weak underneath me, feeling suddenly dizzy. *Get out of here!* my mind screamed. *Get out of the bathroom!*

I finally wrenched my eyes away from the hair and began to move.

And then I froze again.

Because there was someone standing behind me.

A child.

A child wearing a gas mask.

She had long black hair and wore an old, collared blue dress. I couldn't see any part of her face—only the bug-like eyes of the gas mask that reflected the fluorescent lights. The world tilted around me.

I left everything there and raced out of the bathroom, blindly running down the dark hallway, my feet pounding against the linoleum. I approached the corner—

No.

Something poked out from behind the corner. Shoes. Shiny, black Mary Jane shoes. And above them, a lock of black hair poking out, and the long snout of a gas mask.

I skidded to a stop and spun around, running the opposite way. In between my heavy footsteps, I heard light, quick ones. Like she was running after me.

No. Please don't catch me. Please.

Behind me, I heard a giggle. It sounded muffled, as if coming from within the gas mask. But I didn't dare turn around.

I dodged into one of the classrooms and slammed the door shut behind me. Then I peered out the narrow glass window into the dark hallway.

The footsteps grew louder. My entire body shook as I leaned against the door, keeping it shut. I held my breath as the footsteps got louder—

All the air sucked out of my lungs as I saw the small, four-foot-tall silhouette run past the window.

The footsteps receded. I shut my eyes tight, panting, trying to shake off what I'd just seen. I kept repeating to myself: *the rules said they do a sweep of the school. There's no way a kid could be in here. And even if there were a kid in here, they'd be crying out for help or something. They wouldn't just be running around the dark school in a gas mask.*

Whatever was out there... it wasn't a kid.

It was something *else*.

I took another breath in, and another breath out. I don't know how long I stood there, leaning against the wall, trying to process everything. The kid was burned into my brain—the horrifying gas mask obscuring her face, her shiny Mary Janes. What the hell was going on?

I finally pulled my body away from the door and opened my eyes.

I was in a classroom I hadn't been in before. This one was decorated strangely—the colors were all faded, beige and sepia tones. I looked up to see a bulletin board on the nearby wall. The sign above it read **NEWS.**

But the newspaper clippings and photographs pinned there were anything but new.

There was a photo of Dwight D. Eisenhower and Richard Nixon, smiling at a podium. An article with the headline: **Russia Launches Sputnik I.** I checked the date on the clipping, and my heart dropped as I read the year: *1957.*

What the hell...

I tore my eyes away from the bulletin board—and froze.

The classroom was no longer empty.

At every single desk sat a child wearing a gas mask. There was a teacher, too—a woman with a 1950s-style dress and a piece of chalk in her hand—wearing a gas mask. Every single person was turned to look at me, bug-eyes of their masks glinting in the dim light.

This can't be real.

I ran to the door. Turned the knob. It wouldn't turn.

No. Please let me out. Please.

I slammed my entire body against the door. It shuddered on its frame, but didn't open.

A footstep sounded behind me. I wheeled around to see the girl—the girl with the long dark hair—standing right behind me. She looked up at me. I saw my own terrified reflection in the glass eyes of her mask.

"What do you want?!" I screamed.

The girl tilted her head, looking up at me.

"*Get away from me!*"

In an instant, the entire classroom was on their feet. A thunder of little footsteps, as they all swarmed around me, the teacher looming behind them. The entire classroom shook underneath their feet. They all stared at me through their gas masks, my terrified face reflected back at me dozens of times.

"*HELP!*" I screamed. My voice echoed in the tiny room. I frantically twisting the door knob behind me. The children stared at me, silently, canting their heads as if observing me intently.

As if deciding what to do with me.

And then, suddenly, I remembered—*the salt.*

I knew from somewhere that salt was supposed to stop ghosts, or spirits, or demons—I couldn't even remember which. But I pulled a salt packet out of my pocket, ripped it open, and flung it at them.

I heard a *crack,* then a rumble like thunder, shaking the entire room.

And in the blink of an eye, they disappeared.

I was standing in an empty classroom.

The silence was deafening. I reached behind and turned the doorknob—it gave, and the door swung open.

I burst into the hallway—and it was only then that I realized I'd been in Classroom Seven. The clock on the wall read twelve minutes after midnight.

I'd broken one of the rules.

I ran as fast as I could down the hallway. Past the open locker. Past the dimly-lit computer lab, monitors flashing asynchronously in my peripheral vision. I didn't stop running until I saw the glowing red EXIT sign. I shoved my body against the doors and they gave way; then I was gasping in the cold air, under a sky full of stars.

I got in my car, sped away from Shady Oaks Elementary, and never looked back.

I got several calls from an unknown number the next day. I figured it was probably someone from the school, asking where I was. But I didn't answer.

When I listened to the voicemails, however, no one spoke. All I heard was slow, ragged, muffled breathing.

Like someone breathing through a gas mask.

I spent hours at the computer, researching everything. Trying to figure out what actually happened. And after hours and hours of searching, I was able to piece together a story.

Shady Oaks Elementary conducted gas mask drills during the 1950s, like many American schools during the Cold War. Unfortunately, a girl in the third grade got a faulty mask, and she'd tragically passed away.

Ever since then, students have periodically gone

missing from Shady Oaks Elementary. The school generates so much income, however, the headmaster and teachers cover it up. They continue onward as if nothing has happened, more than happy to take twenty thousand dollars from each student.

I also found anonymous accounts from former students and teachers of Shady Oaks Elementary, talking about their own experiences. Some described experiences similar to my own—teachers walking into a classroom, and realizing it was their childhood classroom. Students using the computer lab and seeing strange images on the monitors, hearing strange sounds. The students that had gone missing were always last seen in the library, where the girl in the gas mask had passed away. The school was continually paying contractors to add more and more layers of drywall over the part of the library where she'd passed away, hoping to seal up her vengeful spirit forever.

The most damning piece of evidence I came across, however, was just a small detail.

One post mentioned the locker of the girl in the gas mask. The one she'd used before she died.

It was Locker #108.

The same locker the rules had told me to avoid.

THE HEAD IN MY FRIDGE

From a distance, the town of Dawn Peak, Colorado looks beautiful enough to be on a postcard. Snow-capped mountains, towering pines, cabins sending plumes of smoke into the sky. It's like living in a painting or a dream.

Except for the murders.

We found the first body in March, just as the ice began to thaw. A man in his 40s, found off one of the many hiking trails up Mt. Solitude. We assumed it was just a hiker who lost his way—until we found the second body.

This body was missing its head, which obviously ruled out exposure or natural causes.

We were dealing with murder.

And as the sheriff of this Podunk town, it was my job to find out who did it. I naively thought our investigation was making progress—I'd ruled out several suspects, and was moving methodically down the list. We were gathering more evidence. No smoking gun yet, but the investigation was certainly moving along.

On the night of June 2nd, however, everything changed.

It was a quiet night. My teenage sons were staying at my ex-wife's for the weekend, leaving me in an empty house. I'd spent the day catching up on soap operas. Yeah, I know it's not a good look for the town sheriff to watch soap operas, especially in the middle of a murder investigation. But in other words, it was a completely ordinary Sunday.

When it got to be around 8 o'clock, I got hungry. And when I checked the fridge, there was nothing to eat.

So I went down to the basement.

I have a spare fridge down there. I like to buy meat when it's on sale and store it down there, along with some spare beer. My ex-wife always thought it was dumb. She told me the money I spent in electricity outweighed the savings. I disagreed.

Now she didn't get a say.

I walked down the stairs. The familiar damp, musty smell hit my nostrils. When I got to the bottom, I reached up for the cord to turn the light on—but when I pulled it, nothing happened.

Bulb's out already? I thought.

I just replaced it a few weeks ago...

I turned my phone's flashlight on and looked up. The light bulb, strangely, had been shattered.

Oh, damn. Now I was out a buck fifty. Stupid Dawn Peak and its stupid temperature fluctuations. Shattered glass like it was nothing.

I shook my head, made a mental note to replace the light bulb, and continued my way through the dark basement towards the fridge.

Honestly, seeing the refrigerator in this dim light, maybe my ex-wife was right. It was an eyesore, grimy and beat up, with a big dent from when the boys hit it with a baseball. I'd got it at a yard sale years ago for cheap, but maybe it was time for it to go to the big landfill in the sky.

I sighed and yanked the fridge open.

Then I froze.

There was... *something*... poking up over the cans of beer. Something dark. Something that looked like...

Hair?

My first thought was a mouse had somehow gotten into the fridge. I'd had a few of them down here. And I hadn't opened this fridge in a week or so... how long had it been there?

Stomach turning, I pushed the cans of beer out of the way. But as soon as I got a glimpse of what was behind them, I stumbled back.

It wasn't a mouse.

It was a human head in my fridge.

Hands shaking, I reached out and slowly pushed the cans further away. Hoping that I was wrong. But I wasn't: it was, undeniably, a human head.

It appeared to be a man's head. Maybe 40s, though the harsh fridge light probably made him look older than he was. Most likely Caucasian, although his skin had a deathly blue pallor that made it hard to tell for sure.

From those facts alone, he was a match for our victim.

I stared at the face, frozen. His hair, slightly wavy, was matted to his face with condensation. His eyes were closed, and his mouth hung slightly open. There was no blood under the head, but there was water, as if...

The head had been frozen.

My heart pounded in my chest. We'd found the body two months ago. What if the killer had kept the head all this time, in his freezer, and now... broke into my house and put it in my fridge?

I swept my flashlight around the basement. But it was empty. He must've put it here days ago—and I was just finding it now.

But why?

To frame me?

Maybe I'm getting close to catching him. The next few suspects I'm bringing in for questioning... maybe one of them is him. And he wants to put an end to it. To me.

I slammed the door shut, pulled out my phone, and dialed the police station. But as I was about to press the call button, my hand froze.

This doesn't look good, Johnny.

A murder victim's head in your fridge.

All the evidence we had so far was circumstantial. There was no DNA evidence—it had been washed away with the spring rains. And the body was too badly decomposed to pinpoint time of death. Which meant I couldn't be exonerated with an alibi.

And with my history...

I'd been in trouble with the department. I'd accidentally bungled the evidence on the Sara Mansford case a few years back, which led some people in town to believe I was guilty. Thankfully, we were able to eventually extract DNA from under her fingernails, but I still vividly remember the fallout. A twenties-something girl who thought she was the next Nancy Grace went on TikTok and began posting all this "proof" that I'd done it. Detailing how I'd contaminated evidence.

If something "looks bad," it spreads like wildfire.

And then you're tried in the court of public opinion.

I could see the headlines now, dancing before

my eyes. *Murder victim's head found in sheriff's secret basement fridge.*

Could I really prove myself innocent?

In a case with such little evidence?

No. The better plan would be to get rid of it. Take the head back out to the woods, toss it deep in there, where it might never be found. No one would trace it back to me.

I'd make sure of that.

I ran back up the stairs. Pulled gloves on, so my prints wouldn't be found. Then I grabbed a paper bag and a cardboard box. I ran back down the stairs and yanked the fridge open.

I reached in and grabbed the head.

The skin was cold through my gloves. The hair looked so real, so human, matted in half-curls to his pale forehead. I swallowed back a wave of nausea and slowly, carefully, lowered it into the paper bag. Then I put it inside the cardboard box and folded the flaps down for good measure.

No one would see that it was a head. *No one.*

I carried it back up the stairs, swallowing down another wave of nausea. The head rolled around inside the box with each step. I walked out into the driveway, my entire body shaking. *Am I really doing this?* I shook my head. *I have to. I have no choice.* The lights were on across the street—hopefully they weren't watching.

What if they have a doorbell camera? And it's recording me right now?

I shook off my thoughts and quickly put the box in the backseat.

Then I began the drive to the state park. It was only about five miles down the road. I'd walk a half mile into the woods or so and toss it. Maybe cover it with a layer of leaves and sticks. Then I'd take these memories and lock them away, deep inside my mind. If I was ever questioned about it—I never found a head. I never disposed of it in the woods.

The gravel crunched under my tires. I pulled into the first parking space, at the trailhead, and cut the headlights. Then I just sat there, staring into the darkness.

Am I really going to do this?

Am I really going to go against everything I believe in?

What if this head could lead us to the killer?

My mind raced. Sweat stuck my shirt to my back. I stared out into the dark forest—and then, I was jolted out of my thoughts by a loud *thump*.

Coming from the backseat.

I whipped around. Oh, it was just the box. The box with the head. It had fallen onto the floor—it must've been teetering on the edge of the seat, or something. One of the flaps hung open, now, and the brown paper bag was visible in the darkness.

Except the paper bag... it was sticking to the

contours of his face. Almost like... he'd opened his mouth and sucked in a breath, pulling the brown paper taut against his face.

That's ridiculous, I told myself. *He's dead. He can't breathe.*

I reached back and slowly tugged the paper bag off the head—almost expecting to see his head staring back at me, alive. But, of course, he was as pale and dead as before.

But now, seeing his face again, a pang of guilt hit me.

I can't do this.
This man had a life. Maybe a family, worried sick.
I can't do it.

I backed out of the parking lot and drove back to my house. I brought the box back down to the basement. First thing tomorrow, I'd bring it down to the station. I'd tell them the truth—that someone put it there. That I had nothing to do with the murder. And if they didn't believe me... well, I'd have to deal with that on my own.

Still wearing my gloves, I put the head back in the fridge. Top shelf, where I'd found it. Facing away from me. Then I peeled off the gloves, stashed the bag and box under the workshop bench. Nobody had to know about my failed attempt to dispose of it.

I walked back to the fridge, to shut the door.
I froze.

The head had been turned. It was no longer facing me—it was turned to the side. His profile—his large nose, his chiseled jaw—was starkly illuminated in the light of the fridge.

There's no way. No way.

But then a horrible thought dawned on me.

The murderer. What if he's in here with me, right now?

What if he never left?

What if he turned the head just to taunt me?

I wheeled around, holding my phone high, sweeping the flashlight beam across the basement. "Hey!" I shouted, my voice echoing off the cement walls. "I know you're in here!"

Nothing.

"I got a gun!"

Nothing.

Being sheriff and all, I probably should've held my ground until the intruder stepped forward. But instead, I backed towards the stairs. I wouldn't turn my back on the murderer. I wouldn't.

I was only a few steps away when I heard something.

A hiss of breath.

"I hear you!" I shouted. "I hear you breathing!"

Silence.

And then the *hiss* again.

But it was coming from the middle of the room.

Where the refrigerator stood.

What the hell? The flashlight's beam shook as my hand trembled. I stood there, frozen—and then the *hissing* sounded again. But this time, it sounded more like a raspy wheeze.

"Come out here, you coward!" I shouted, my voice shaking.

Whispers.

Frantic, hurried whispers. Too quiet to make out the words. Echoing against the cement walls.

I lifted the flashlight, staring at the shadow behind the refrigerator. It was a few inches away from the wall—no one could fit behind there, right? But there was no other explanation. Someone was whispering in my basement, and it certainly wasn't the dead guy.

But I was wrong.

The head's lips were moving. I could see it, clearly, in the harsh white light of the flashlight.

The head in the fridge... was whispering to me.

No way. This is a dream. This can't be happening. I pinched myself. I checked my watch a few times. Nothing indicated I was dreaming. The whispers continued.

I wasn't dreaming. This was real.

I stared at the head, frozen. Watching the lips move frantically, forming whispers that bounced off the cement walls and then faded into the darkness of my basement.

And then I realized.

Ezra.

My fourteen-year-old son. A few years ago, he was *obsessed* with playing pranks on me. Hasn't done a good one in a few years, but this could absolutely be his doing. The head could be a Halloween decoration; one of those fancy animatronic ones that moves and speaks. I still vividly remember the time he put a fake spilled Starbucks coffee right on top of my new computer.

And an animatronic head in the fridge would scare me a lot more than that.

Sure, the head looked and felt real. But so would an expensive prop. I turned the flashlight off on my phone and dialed Ezra. He picked up after three rings.

"I found the head," I told him. "Ha ha. Very funny."

"...What are you talking about?" he replied.

And I could tell. From the confusion in his voice, it was obvious. He didn't do this. My kid's a lot of things, but he's not a good liar.

I ended the call. But when I looked back at the fridge, I nearly fainted.

The head was now facing me again.

I stepped forward, my entire body trembling.

This close, I could see that it was far too realistic to be a Halloween prop. Even though the eyes were closed, I could see movement under the eyelids. As if the man were moving his eyes frantically back and forth. And the lips were moving to form words—it wasn't some motor under the jaw that was opening and closing the jaw.

I froze there, staring at the head.

It's real.

And then I realized what he was saying. It was the same five words, repeated over and over again.

"*The man with the serpent. The man with the serpent.*"

I came to my senses. I slammed the fridge door shut and ran back up the stairs. Then I slid the chain lock over the basement door. Not like that thing could move. Unless it could grow insect legs like that one guy's head in the movie *The Thing* and scuttle up the stairs.

I shuddered.

Then I ran into the kitchen. I pulled out a bottle of whiskey and poured myself a shot. My hands were shaking so much, half of it sloshed onto the counter.

It's not my imagination, and it's not a prop. What does that leave, then? Back during my training, I remembered learning about how bodies can move after they're dead. Just little muscle twitches and things like that. Echoes of life. The whispered words almost felt like that: like some glitchy echo, left behind. Whispering the same words, over and over, destined to repeat them for eternity.

The man with the serpent.

It had to be the head of the man we found. The age and race seemed to match. Was that supposed to be some sort of clue? The man with the serpent? Was that who killed him?

I took another sip of whiskey.

It didn't matter. Tomorrow I'd take it down to the station and explain everything. Maybe forensics could lift some prints off it. Maybe we could get started on identifying him, finding his family, and figuring out who did this to him.

But what if everything flipped upside-down, like the Sara Mansford thing?

I needed proof I had nothing to do with this.

And then I got an idea.

I had two security cameras. One at my back door, and one at my front. I would be able to see who put the head in my fridge, unless they'd broken in through a side window.

The last time I used the fridge was last Thursday, I think. When I got some kielbasa and a beer and watched the season thirty-two finale of Days of Our Lives. So I painstakingly went through each video between Thursday and tonight.

But none of the videos showed anything out of the ordinary. Just me coming and going from work, and a few deliveries.

I downed the rest of the whiskey. And then as I sat there, staring at the wall, I heard it.

A dull *thump, thump, thump* coming from the basement.

I froze. I pictured the head, pulling itself out of the fridge with spider-like legs poking out from under its chin. Scuttling across the floor. Leaping up the stairs.

I ran upstairs and I got my gun. Then I positioned myself at the end of the hallway, gun trained on the door.

Thump, thump, thump.

I raised the gun—

And then I heard water rushing through the pipes.

Of course. I lowered my gun. Those stupid pipes made that sound all the time—but somehow my brain jumped directly to *murderous spider head.* Man, I was really working myself up over here.

I let out a laugh and sat back down, getting comfortable. I wasn't comfortable enough to go to sleep upstairs, but I'd just hang out here, watching the door. And then as soon as dawn came I'd drag that thing over to the station and let them deal with whatever crazy black magic stuff this was.

But I must have fallen asleep at some point, because I woke up with a start. As I faded back into consciousness, I realized what had woken me up.

There were screams coming from the basement.

Horrible, blood-curdling screams of pain.

I grabbed the gun and ran over to the basement

door. Yanked it open and ran down the stairs, gun trained ahead of me. The screaming got louder.

I froze at the bottom.

The screaming was coming from inside the refrigerator.

No, no, no.

I approached slowly, gun aimed at the refrigerator door. Then I took a deep breath, curled my fingers around the handle, and yanked it open.

The head had fallen over.

It was lying on its side, facing away from me. And as soon as I'd opened the door, it had stopped screaming.

He... it... whatever it was, had resumed whispering. *"The man with the serpent,"* over and over, like a broken record. I should've just closed the door—but my nerves were shot. I wasn't going to sit here, terrified in my own home.

I'm the SHERIFF. I'm better than this.

I'm going to take care of this thing once and for all.

So I did something that was incredibly stupid.

I walked over to the plastic bin a few feet away. Popped open the lid and pulled out an old T-shirt. Hands shaking, I gingerly reached into the refrigerator and draped the T-shirt over the head. I didn't want to see what happened next.

If I wasn't sleep deprived and in panic mode, I would've realized that the bullet would be traced back to my gun. That it would implicate me in the murder.

But in the moment, I would do *anything* to get that head to shut up.

I stepped back and raised my gun. Flicked the safety off, finger poised on the trigger. I sucked in a breath—

And then I froze.

I watched in horror as the shape under the T-shirt begin to move. The head was somehow turning itself over.

I backed away. *This can't be happening. This can't be—*

Thump!

The head rolled forward. The T-shirt slid off his face.

He was staring *right at me.*

Pale blue eyes, slightly cloudy from rot and death. Staring right at me.

The gun shook wildly in my hands as I pointed it at him. "What do you want?" I shouted.

I didn't expect him to respond. But he did. Something like a smile flickered over his face, and then he replied, in a raspy, grating whisper:

"*Are you doing your job, sheriff?*"

I opened my mouth to reply, but no sound came out.

"*Or are you just leaving me here to rot?*"

My legs shook underneath me. "I'm trying to

find who killed you," I choked out. "I'm trying my best—"

"*I gave you a clue. But you did not take it.*"

My heart was pounding. I felt weak. I took a step back, then another. "If you know who killed you, tell me."

"*The man with the serpent.*"

"What did he look like? His height? Age? Anything?"

The head grew agitated. He began to chant, frantically, his raspy voice cutting into each syllable—

"*The man with the serpent! The man with the serpent!*"

Panic took over. I ran. I ran as fast as I could to the basement stairs, leaving the fridge hanging wide open.

Raspy shouts sounded behind me.

"*THE MAN WITH THE SERPENT!*"

"*THE MAN WITH THE SERPENT!*"

He sounded angry. *Really* angry. I didn't turn around—I just scrambled up the stairs, trying to keep myself from collapsing. I slammed the door shut, slid the chain lock, and stumbled over to the couch.

Then I hung my head in my hands, somewhere between screaming and sobbing.

This can't be real.

What is happening to me?

A dull thump came from downstairs.

This time, it wasn't the pipes.

Has he... somehow... rolled himself out of the refrigerator?

A wave of nausea washed over me. I ran over to the sink and began to throw up. *This is too much.* I had to call somebody. Even if it meant I was added to the suspect list, even if it meant trashing my reputation in this town. Even if I got arrested —*anything* would be better than being trapped in this house with this head.

I pulled out my phone and called the station. Officer Johnson, one of the younger guys on the force, picked up.

"There's something in my house," I choked out, unsure how else to word it. "I need somebody to come out immediately."

"Sheriff Garland, are you okay?"

"There's something out in my house," I just repeated. "I can't, I just need somebody to come out here, okay?"

I hung up the phone. I thought I heard more sound from downstairs, but it was hard to tell if it was just the house settling, or my imagination. I went into the living room, the furthest room from the basement door, and waited for the cops to arrive.

Johnson showed up a few minutes later with Officer Hernandez. The two of them looked visibly concerned when I opened the door. "Please, just come in," I choked out, motioning them inside.

They kept asking me what was going on, but I couldn't answer. I knew if I told them, they wouldn't believe me. Best if they just saw it for themselves. I led them to the basement door, unlocked it, swung it open.

"Someone's down there," I whispered.

Johnson and Hernandez exchanged a glance. Then they drew their guns and started down the stairs. I listened to their footfalls, waiting for them to reach the bottom.

Then I followed.

I didn't hear anything as I descended the stairs. When I got to the bottom, I saw why. The fridge was hanging open—but it was empty. A thin trail of water stained the cement floor, leading away from the fridge.

The head was gone.

"No. It was *right there,*" I said, pointing to the fridge.

"What... was right there?" Hernandez asked.

I shook my head. "Nevermind."

They would never believe me, without seeing it for themselves.

Hernandez shrugged at Johnson. Then they scanned the basement, guns drawn. They searched the entire thing, but there was no one there.

Well, there was no *person* there. There were still

plenty of hiding places they hadn't checked that would perfectly fit a human head.

"There's no one here," Hernandez said, putting her gun away.

I didn't reply. Instead, I shoved the pile of boxes aside, looking behind them. Pulled up a pile of clothes and looked under them. Grabbed a cardboard box labeled "Holiday Decorations" and yanked it open. Hernandez quirked an eyebrow at me.

"No man's going to fit in there, Sheriff."

"I... I know..."

"Come on," Johnson said. "Let's check the rest of the house."

I stood there, frozen. The head had to be here, somewhere. But it was impossible to search the entire basement for it before they left. So many cardboard boxes, so many nooks and crannies. Unless I admitted to them that we were looking for a severed head instead of a man, I was stuck.

I stayed behind in the basement as they searched the main floor. But nothing was there. After ten minutes, the officers called down, and I went back upstairs. I locked the door and thanked them for coming by.

I decided I was done. I went upstairs and got in bed. I needed sleep, desperately. Maybe in the morning I'd find it and get rid of it, once and for all.

Maybe I'd never find it—maybe it somehow escaped into the night, the same way it came.

I closed my eyes and pulled the blanket up to my neck. *The man with the serpent,* the voice echoed in my brain. His pale dead eyes flashed through my mind.

I tried to picture something else, anything else: sandy shores, rolling hills, a meadow of flowers. It would be nice to take a vacation. *Maybe I should, soon. Maybe to the Keys again.* We hadn't been there since the boys were young. Maybe I'd take the boys. And leave my ex-wife out of the entire thing...

Just as I was about to drift off, a soft thump sounded from the other end of the room.

I sat bolt upright in the darkness. Straining my ears to listen.

And then I heard it.

"The man with the serpent," a whisper said from the foot of my bed.

I screamed.

I reached over and turned on the lamp. There, at the foot of the bed, was the head. Ashen gray skin. Dark hair matted to its face. Bright blue eyes, staring at me, not blinking.

And below his neck, this time, I saw something. A body—but shimmering, translucent, wispy like smoke.

"You are not even trying," he rasped.

"Please, I—"

A smoky hand reached out and grabbed my ankle. Hot pain shot up my leg. "Let go!" I screamed. "Let go of me!"

"Not until you find who did this to me!"

I kicked hard. The grip loosened for a second, and I scrambled out of the room. I ran down the stairs, out of the house. Got in the car and floored it. I would drive a thousand miles to get away from that thing. Whatever it took. I glanced in the rearview mirror, half-expecting to see his face staring back at me; but I was alone.

I did drive for a while. But as the sun peeked over the mountains, I realized what I had to do. This head, this spirit, wouldn't rest. I had to find the man with the serpent.

I got to the station before anyone else. Poured myself a cup of coffee, then another. I pored over the list of suspects. Brought up the mugshots, stalked them online.

Finally, I found him.

A man from the next town over, with a tattoo of a snake coiling around his bicep.

I didn't have enough to arrest him, but I spent the entire day trying to collect evidence. I'd bring him in for questioning in a few days, try to catch him in a lie, try to get enough to subpoena phone records. And I put in another request to forensics, to try and lift fingerprints off the victim's body again.

I won't stop until I get this guy. Not out of altruism, but because the last thing I want to come home to is a severed head.

That's even worse than coming home to my ex-wife.

And even though I was shaking on the drive home that evening, since I hadn't made an arrest yet, it seemed like the spirit was satisfied with my progress. Because when I got home, there was no trace of the head anywhere.

Except for a thin trail of water leading out the back door.

THERE IS SOMETHING HORRIBLE IN THE BIOHAZARD WASTE BAGS AT MY WORKPLACE

It was 6:00 on a Friday, and Dr. Gruber was asking me to stay late.

"The biomedical waste *needs* to be picked up tonight. That stuff can't sit here all weekend."

With all due respect, Dr. Gruber, that's not my fucking problem.

"Can you stay until they come pick it up?"

Oh, no, no.

"I'll pay you overtime. Overtime and a half."

Fuck...

"Okay. But if they're not here by 8, I'm leaving."

"Thank you. So, so much."

Being in an OB/GYN office was the last place I'd want to be on a weekend night. Well, not the *last* place—being in a tent in the Ozarks, leaking rain, in the middle of bear country, with no working toilets for miles was worse. Like our five year anniversary trip.

But this office was probably the next worst thing.

Waiting for the biohazard disposal guys was even worse. Because now I was picturing all the... stuff... contained in those bags. Oh no, it wasn't just needles and swabs. We just had a woman come in last week, six days postpartum, complaining of a "golf-ball-sized blood clot hanging out of her vagina."

Her description was, unfortunately, *extremely* accurate.

So, anyway. Me. And the nasty stuff. All alone in the office.

At least we had Wi-Fi.

I sat down at the front desk and pulled out my phone, scrolling aimlessly through TikTok. But only a few minutes had gone by when I heard a door slam.

From somewhere *inside* the office.

I stood up, clutching my phone. "Hello?"

I scanned the hallway, leading to the exam rooms. All the doors were open, lights on, except for one.

Huh. Maybe the medical waste guy is already here?

I'd gone to my car to get my phone charger, about ten minutes ago. Maybe he'd somehow come in when I was out. I hadn't locked up the office yet —maybe he let himself in.

I walked down the hallway and stood outside the door. "Who's there?" I called.

Silence.

I turned the knob and slowly, *slowly* pushed the door open.

No one was there. The bed was empty, clean paper pulled down over the upholstery. The fluorescent light flickered lazily overhead. A few drops of water dripped from the tap. I sighed, turned the tap all the way off, and walked back over to the front desk. Plopped down in the chair, pulled up TikTok.

But a few minutes later, I heard something else.

A little *thump,* barely audible.

Coming from the waiting room.

I frowned, stood up, and looked through the glass. But the waiting room was empty. Everything was as it should be: the fake ficus in the corner, the gross beige chairs, the splattery modern art hanging on the walls.

I sighed and called the number Dr. Gruber had left for the waste removal guys. They assured me that they would be here within the hour. Which meant we'd still make our eight o'clock reservation.

Cool. I'd expected this to turn into a multi-hour disaster, but it seemed like people were being competent, for once.

I headed to the bathroom to fix my makeup.

My husband and I had planned a date night tonight. We'd been empty nesters for a month now, with my youngest finally flying the coop and moving upstate. Don't get me wrong—I love my kids to death—but after twenty years of three boys trampling through the house, I needed a break.

I leaned in close to the mirror and applied an extra layer of eyeliner. Then I texted Rob, letting him know I might be a little late.

Then I lifted the toilet lid to pee—

Oh, *gross.*

The toilet was filled with blood. *For Pete's sake.* People always talk about how men are disgusting, but, *what?!* Not flushing the toilet after you pee with your *period?!*

The entire bathroom stank of metallic blood and something rotten. My stomach lurched. Holding my breath, I leaned over to flush the toilet —and then I ran out of the bathroom as fast as I could.

Gross, gross, gross.

I sat back down at the front desk, eyes shut, breathing in deep breaths of fresh air. Finally, when the nausea subsided, I opened my eyes.

I froze.

The waiting room was no longer empty.

There was a woman, sitting in the far corner, facing away from me. Her long, black hair cascading down the back of the seat. Her legs crossed neatly in front of her.

For some reason, my heart began to pound. I approached the window and slid it open. "Are you from Apex Waste Removal?"

No response.

"We're closed," I called out. "But if you want to make an appointment for next week, I can help you do that."

The woman didn't turn around. She didn't react in any way at all. She just sat there, perfectly still, turned away from me.

Chills ran down my spine. The alarm bells were going off in my head. *Something isn't right.* I ducked away from the window, over to the door between the waiting room and the office, and locked it.

I walked back over to the window. "I'm sorry, we're—"

My breath caught in my throat.

No one was there.

I started to close the window—and that's when I noticed the paper.

It was one of our patient intake forms. The kind we gave to new patients, asking about pre-existing conditions, previous births, etc. But instead of being filled out, there was just one word written in the space for the patient's name.

BEWARE

My throat went dry. *Is that a threat? Beware of*

what? I stood there, tapping my hands on the counter. Then I pulled out my phone and called Rob. "Hey, uh, can you come to my office?" I asked, scanning the waiting room.

"I guess," he replied. "Everything okay?"

"It's nothing," I said, forcing a laugh. "There was just, this woman in the waiting room, and she was kind of... creeping me out a bit. I don't really want to be here alone, so I thought... maybe you could stay here with me, until the waste guys come?"

"Uh, sure," he said. "I'll be there in twenty minutes."

I ended the call, glanced at the door to make sure it was locked—then went back to TikTok, waiting for Rob. After five minutes I decided to get up and stretch a little. As I did, I did a final scan of the waiting room.

That's when I realized the woman had never left.

She was crouched behind the fake ficus. Dark hair falling over her face, blending with the shadows. Hands pressed to the floor in a sort of leap frog crouch. Still as a statue. Completely naked.

What the fuck what the actual fuck.

I ran. I ran down the hallway, back into the office, towards the exam rooms. Raced into EXAM ROOM 2, slammed the door shut, and wedged the chair against it.

I cowered against the back wall and pulled out my phone.

"*She's still here!*" I whispered when Rob picked up. "*She's STILL HERE!*"

"What—are you okay?"

"I'm locked in an exam room—but—*call the police*—there's something really wrong, I think she—"

My voice was cut off by a strange, wet *splat* sound.

Coming from inside the room.

The phone fell out of my hand.

I turned towards the direction of the sound.

What the...

My mind went blank as I stared at the BIOHAZARD WASTE bag hanging on the wall.

It was moving. Something was *moving* inside the bag.

My stomach turned as I pictured a rat climbing inside, attracted by the smell of blood and waste.

But it couldn't be. Because it looked like protuberances—*fingers?!*—stretching the plastic, testing the strength of the bag. As if trying to get out.

What the fuck what the fuck.

My phone rang on the floor. I scrambled to pick it up. "The police are on their way, okay?" Rob said, his voice panicked. "Just—are you somewhere safe?"

"I'm... I'm still locked in an exam room," I whispered.

THUMP! The entire bag shuddered with motion, slapping against the wall behind it. As if whatever was inside was now wildly thrashing. A wave of nausea and I forced myself to look away, turning towards the exam bed.

Oh, God.

The woman. She was sitting on the bed, turned away from me. Wearing nothing but a hospital gown. Blood trickled down her back, matting her hair. Dripping onto the paper.

I backed away, hitting the wall.

"Please..." I whispered. "Please, don't..."

I didn't expect her to respond. But she did. First, a low whisper, three words:

"Open the bag."

"Please, please don't—"

"Open the bag."

"I can't—"

"OPEN THE BAG!"

Her voice was guttural and low. As if she were talking from vocal cords ripped and ravaged, half-severed. I let out a sob.

Her head began to swivel towards me.

It was only attached to her neck by a thin strip of flesh.

"OPEN THE BAG," she said again. Her cheek, her ear, now visible to me. Her head tilted horribly

wrong on her neck, threatening to slip off at any second.

I reached up with shaking hands towards the biohazard bag. Rob was screaming for me from the phone on the floor, but I couldn't move, couldn't pick it up. All I could do was grab the bag from the wall—it was no longer moving—and pull it open.

No.

Among the used syringes, the cotton swabs—

Was a severed finger.

When I'd stopped screaming, the woman was gone.

The finger belonged to a young woman in her twenties named Erica Howard.

She was a patient of Dr. Gruber's.

A patient who had been inappropriately touched during an exam.

Who had threatened to go to the police.

He had murdered her three days ago. He had placed her remains in various biomedical waste bins inside the office early this morning, before anyone else had arrived. Hoping they would get disposed of with no one noticing.

That's why he was adamant they got disposed of on Friday.

And didn't sit there all weekend.

I'm glad Dr. Gruber is being brought to justice. But I still can't scrub the image out of my head. Of the woman sitting on the exam bed, her head lolling back towards me. Her guttural voice telling me to open the bag.

And the bloody, severed finger.

I changed my mind. I don't want to be an empty-nester anymore. I don't want to be alone in the house when Rob has an errand to run or works late.

I want to be surrounded by as many people as possible, all the time.

I never want to be alone again.

MY GRANDMA ISN'T MY GRANDMA

I haven't seen my grandma in three years. My mom and I moved across the country after the divorce, and we didn't have the money for a plane ticket. (At least, that's what my mom claims. I think it's just because she hates my grandma.)

Well, funny how her attitude magically changed when her boyfriend presented her with plane tickets to Costa Rica. *Ava, your Grandma's so much fun. She'll teach you how to knit. She'll teach you how to bake butterscotch cookies. She's the best!*

She did warn me about something, though.

"Her mind has gotten bad," my mom told me. "She has trouble remembering things... recognizing people."

"Is she gonna be okay?"

"Yeah, but... just be patient with her, okay? And

if she seems really out of it, call Mrs. Dempsey down the street. I put her number in your phone."

"Okay."

"But you're going to have a great time!" my mom said, plastering on a smile. "It's going to be wonderful!"

Two days later I was getting off at Pittsburgh airport. Funny how my mom said I was too young to go to the diner alone with Shireen—*the world is dangerous for a thirteen-year-old girl,* her words—but she had no problem sending me off on a plane alone.

My grandma wasn't great with cell phones—she didn't pick up when I called—but as soon as I got to the pickup line, I saw her silver Subaru Outback at the curb. Grandma stood beside it, smiling widely.

"Grandma!" I said, running up to her.

She didn't open her arms to hug me. She just stood there, looking down at me.

"... Grandma?"

"Hello, dear," she said, after a pause, as if just noticing me for the first time now. "How have you been? I'm so happy to see you."

Then she opened the car door and gestured me inside.

The car smelled like old-person smell. I'm sorry that's mean, but it's true. I crinkled my nose as I pulled on my seatbelt, and she drove us back through the city, out into the Pennsylvanian countryside.

"Get comfortable, dear," Grandma said as she led me inside. The house looked the same as it always did: a little stale, a little outdated, but also oddly comforting compared to the 'minimalistic' style of my mom's house. I glanced at the needlepoint hanging in the foyer, of a large pitcher of lemonade.

"Make yourself at home. You can eat anything you find in the fridge or the pantry," she told me. "Oh! Except, I almost forgot. I do have one rule. The basement is off-limits."

"Why?"

"It's a little dangerous down there, dear. Wouldn't want you getting hurt."

I frowned. The basement had never been off-limits before. It was finished on one side, and she had a bunch of board games and a sofa down there. I liked hanging out down there. It was the only place that didn't smell like old people.

"It wasn't dangerous before," I protested.

"Well, it is now," she said—in a significantly firmer tone. Then her smile went right back on, and she asked me: "Would you like some butterscotch cookies?"

"Yes, please!"

My mom was right—Grandma was kind of fun. I helped her with the cookies, and she told me she'd send me home with the recipe. I did some reading and talked to my friend Shireen on the phone. Then it was bedtime.

Tall and thin, Grandma looked like a ghost as she paced down the dark hallway to her bedroom. "Night-night," she said, poking her head out and giving me a wave.

"G'night, Grandma."

Her blue eyes glinted in the darkness. Then the door snicked shut.

I fell asleep quickly, despite the bed that was a little too soft and the loud cricket outside my window. I woke up with a start, however, and looked at my phone to see it was almost 2 AM.

My throat was parched, so I headed out to the hall bathroom to get some water.

As I walked across the hallway, I noticed Grandma's bedroom door was open.

And as I looked harder...

What the hell?

Grandma was sitting on her bed in her nightgown. Staring out into the hallway, head tilted slightly. Blue eyes glinting in the darkness.

I stopped in my tracks.

"... Grandma?"

Was she... *smiling?*

"Grandma!"

"Ava, is that you?" she called out.

No, she wasn't smiling. At least not anymore.

"Yeah, it's me," I replied, my voice wavering. "Why are you up?"

"I thought I heard something," she replied. "So I was just sitting here to make sure… it was nothing."

I got my water, feeling unsettled. When I got out of the bathroom, Grandma was poking her head out of the doorway again, waving. "Night-night."

"…. Goodnight."

The next day, when I asked her about it, she didn't even seem to remember the interaction.

"I don't remember being up," she said, looking at me. In the sunny light filtering through the window, she looked much less… scary. White hair tied back with a silver barrette, pale wrinkled skin, tired blue eyes. "You saw me up?"

"Yes," I said, firmly.

"Huh." She rose from the seat, still in her nightgown, and shuffled towards the stove. "Would you like pancakes this morning, Alison?"

My heart sank. Alison was my mom's name. "Ava," I corrected, following her into the kitchen.

"Right, of course. Ava." She shook her head. "You're just a spitting image of her, when she was your age. The dark eyebrows, and the curly hair…" She shook her head again. "It's like going back in time."

She made the pancakes in silence. The tines of the fork, hitting the bowl. Another egg *glooping* in, cracked eggshells set by the counter. A sharp sizzle as the viscous batter hit the cast iron pan.

"I have chocolate chips I can add," she said, riffling through the counter. "Oh, wait... these expired a year ago."

"It's fine," I told her.

After breakfast, I thought maybe we'd play a game of Go Fish like old times, or take a walk; but Grandma had other plans. "I'm afraid I'm feeling rather tired," she told me. "Is it okay if I go rest, and you just hang out here?"

"That's fine. I brought my Switch," I told her. "Video games."

"Oh! Okay. That's nice. Well, get me if you need anything, okay?"

I nodded.

I found myself surprised that I was disappointed. I thought I didn't miss all those things we used to do, boring things like playing cards or walking. But I did. *Whatever. I'm here for a whole week,* I told myself, going up to my room. I booted up my Switch and started playing Pokemon.

A few hours went by. When I got hungry, I went back down to the kitchen; but Grandma still wasn't around. *I hope she's okay,* I thought.

I poked around the fridge and found some leftover chicken, dated two days ago. I popped it in the microwave and sat down to eat.

I'd only been eating a few minutes when I heard it.

A scuffing sound.

Coming from the basement.

I got off the couch and walked towards the basement door. *She told me not to go down there.* What was down there, then? Rats? An illegal, exotic pet? *Yeah right.* The scuffing sounds continued; I pressed my ear to the door.

And then I heard it.

"Help me."

Spoken *in my Grandma's voice.*

Every muscle in my body froze. *She must've gotten trapped down there. Maybe she fell down the stairs. That's why I haven't seen her for hours.* I undid the deadbolt and swung the door open. "Grandma?" I called.

The lights were off, but from what little I could see, it didn't look like she was lying at the bottom of the stairs. *Thank God.* "Grandma?" I called again, louder this time.

"Help me."

"I'm co—"

Hands grabbed me from behind and yanked me forcefully back.

The door slammed in my face. Then my grandma was in my face, her eyes wild. *"I told you not to go in the basement!"* she shrieked, so loudly my ears rang.

"I—I heard you down there," I said, my voice trembling.

"No you didn't," she snapped back, her face twisted in this awful, vicious expression of anger I'd never seen before. "I'm right here. I was upstairs lying down when I heard you calling for me. There is no one down there."

"But... but I heard you," I said, tears starting to prickle my eyes.

She just shook her head and walked away.

For the rest of the day, Grandma sat in the living room, knitting. Every time I passed by the basement door, her eyes followed me. I started to feel incredibly uncomfortable. When I went up to my bedroom to talk to Shireen, I could hear her footsteps outside my door. She was trying to be as quiet as possible—her footsteps were slow and light—but I still heard them.

When I came down for dinner, Grandma was all smiles. She served me a dish of warm lasagna, cheese melty and gooey on top, smelling of garlic and onion. "Thanks," I said. It felt like she was trying to make amends for yelling at me.

But when I sat down to eat it, she just *stared* at me.

"Aren't you going to have some?" I asked, hovering the first bite next to my mouth.

"No, it doesn't fit my diet. This is just for you, Alison," she replied.

"Ava," I snapped back.

I set the fork down. This was feeling like all kinds of weird. I stared at my Grandma's face, a chill going down my spine. Her blue eyes were so intense, so cold. She seemed so... *different*... from three years ago.

"What kind of cake did you make me for my ninth birthday?" I asked.

She tilted her head, staring intently. "I don't remember, dear."

"You spent all day on that cake. Of course you remember."

Her mouth became a thin line. She paused. "I don't remember."

"What's my birthday, then?" I pressed.

She blinked. "It's... October, isn't it?"

"September 14th."

"I'm sorry, dear," she finally said, breaking eye contact. "I don't remember things as well as I used to. And I mix up names, and words. It's not because I don't love you."

I stared at her.

And then I forced a fake smile.

"I know, Grandma. I love you."

Then I got up from the table and started up the stairs.

"You haven't finished your lasagna, dear!" Grandma's voice came, from the bottom of the stairs.

"I'm not hungry," I called back.

I hadn't taken a single bite.

"I think my grandma's a skinwalker," I whispered into the phone.

Shireen gasped on the other end. "What?"

"She doesn't remember anything about me. I think she's keeping my real grandma locked away down in the basement."

"What?"

"I heard her voice. Calling for help."

A heavy sigh. Shireen was not the superstitious type. "Are you *sure* you heard her voice from the basement?"

"Yes."

"What are you going to do?"

"I'm going to go down there," I replied. "*Tonight.*"

"Maybe you should just wait for your mom to get back."

"My grandma could be dead by then!"

"Maybe you should call the police."

"What if my grandma tells them I'm a liar, that I made it all up? Are they going to believe her, or a thirteen year old girl?"

"I still think you shouldn't go down there."

"Well, I'm gonna."

"Okay, well, give me your address or something. If you don't call me back, I'll call the police."

"Good idea."

I gave her my address, she tried to talk me out of it for another ten minutes, and then I hung up. Then I swung the door open and crept out into the hallway.

Silence. Darkness under Grandma's (or Not-Grandma's) door.

I was safe.

I tiptoed down the stairs and walked over to the basement door. Then I waited for a few minutes, to make sure Not-Grandma wasn't following me.

Silence.

I slowly, quietly, slid the deadbolt. Then I swung the door open, creaking slightly on its hinges. I winced, hoping that didn't wake her up.

No scuffing sounds. No voice, calling for help.

Maybe she's already—

I swallowed the thought and started down the stairs.

The light didn't seem to work, but I had my phone with me. The flashlight illuminated each step beneath me. I slowly made my way down—when my feet hit the cold, concrete bottom, I swung the light around.

All the blood drained out of my face.

Sitting on the floor, chained to a support pole,

was my grandma. Her head hung limply in front of her, white curls hanging over her face.

"Grandma!" I called, my throat tightening.

I hope she isn't already—

Grandma lifted her head.

The phone fell out of my hands.

Her face. There was something horribly wrong with her face. Pure-white eyes. A wide smile, full of pointed teeth. Skin that seemed to slough off her face in patches, revealing bone beneath.

No. No, no, no—

A horrible cracking sound filled the air.

I watched, in horror, as the *thing* transformed. Bones twisted and contorted. The face opened its mouth in a silent scream. And then... I was staring at *myself* chained to the post, white eyes fading to match my brown ones.

It cocked its head.

"Hello," it said in a voice that matched my own.

I let out a scream.

And then Grandma—real Grandma, from upstairs, not this horrible thing—was grabbing me and shoving me up the stairs. The door slammed shut and I found myself on the floor, panting, looking up at her.

"What did I tell you?! *Don't go in the basement!*"

"What... Grandma..." I choked out.

She double-checked the door was locked, then led me to the kitchen.

"That *thing* showed up a year ago," she told me, as she pulled out my leftover, now congealed, piece of lasagna from the fridge. She draped a thin blanket over my shoulders and sat down across from me. "At first, it took the appearance of an old friend of mine. I let it in. I fed it. Not just food," she said, glancing down at the lasagna in front of me, still uneaten. "It started eating my memories."

"How…"

"I don't know how. But I found myself forgetting simple things. Names. Dates. Birthdays. And then one day, I woke up to the thing… looking just like me. I don't think it was aware that I would not respond well to a person looking exactly like me. I tricked it into the basement by pretending to relive a memory of the basement being a very important place, over and over again. It eventually 'ate' that memory, and went down there. I locked it in. With the help of someone I met online, someone who believed me, I was able to chain it to the post. And I'm keeping it there so it can't hurt anyone else."

I stared at her.

"If you knew you had this dangerous thing in your basement, why did you let me stay here?"

"I missed you, and I foolishly thought you'd listen to me."

Scuffling sounds came from beneath us. And then I heard my own voice, reverberating through the floor: *"HELP ME! GET BACK DOWN HERE AND HELP ME!"*

"Will it eat my memories, too?" I whispered.

"No. It needs physical contact for that."

Our talk was interrupted by three short knocks on the door—and that's when I realized I never called Shireen back.

And couldn't, because my phone was at the bottom of the basement stairs, down there with *it*.

"Uh, I'll take care of this," I told her, getting up from the kitchen table.

Thankfully, the police bought my tale, and because I didn't let them in, didn't hear the clone of me screaming the basement.

Then I used Grandma's old computer to send Shireen an email.

There's still the matter of the thing in the basement, of course. But that's another problem for another day.

For now, I'm going to eat some lasagna, and then go straight to bed.

And Mom was right—

My Grandma *is* fun.

POSTPARTUM DECAY

My nose is four millimeters shorter than it used to be.

I measured it. I took a ruler and pressed it against my cheek, hard, until the skin bloomed pink. I did it a second time, and then a third, just to be sure.

It was shorter.

No one else noticed. Not even my husband. But I did. Every time I went into the bathroom, I recognized the woman in the mirror less and less. My face was changing, gradually, right before my eyes.

And it all started with the birth of my daughter.

The very first thing was the hair loss. I'd been warned on mommy forums about the hairpocalypse. How much it sheds once those pregnancy hormones aren't pumping through your body. Every time I showered, big, tangled clumps fell through my fingers and stuck to the drain.

The hair loss I expected. The other changes, initially, were also par for the course. My feet were bigger. My hips were wider, not because of fat, but because the bones had spread apart when I gave birth. I even looked different *down there.*

Your body is just different after pregnancy, everyone told me. *It just is.*

But as the weeks went on—as my little baby giggled and smiled and met her milestones—I met milestones, too. My nose began to shorten, like someone was taking a razor to it in the middle of the night and nicking off layers of skin. The birthmark under my right eye began to fade.

And I began to lose weight.

Most mothers would be happy about that. But I was losing it fast—too fast. It almost seemed like with each pound Ava gained, I lost one. At her three-month checkup, when she tipped the scales at thirteen pounds, I was the lightest I'd ever been. One-hundred seventeen.

"You're not eating enough," my husband said.

"Yes, I am."

"Maddie..." he said, and his eyes looked sad. "Are you lying to me?"

I understood the implication. I'd suffered from

an eating disorder for several years. Hiding food in my napkin at the table. Packing my pockets full of coins when he forced me to step on the scale. He wasn't wrong to question me, but I resented it all the same.

"I swear. I'm telling the truth."

"Maybe you should stop nursing, then," he said, after a pause.

"Yeah. I think I will."

I knew breast milk was the best, with all the antibodies and IQ-boosting proteins and whatnot, but I needed to look out for myself, too. Every night, I held Ava with thinner, bonier arms. Soon I'd be nothing more than a skeleton.

"I will," I repeated.

He hugged me and kissed me and told me he loved me, but it felt hollow.

———

Around the time Ava was six months old, and sitting up on her own, the fingerprint reader on my phone stopped working. At first, I blamed the phone. It was old, scuffed, and cracked after all, because all our expendable income now went to diapers and formula instead of new phones.

But then I looked down at my hands—and I realized the phone wasn't the problem.

The pads of my fingertips were entirely smooth.

Like they'd been badly burned. Like the grooves had been carefully sanded down into nothingness. I stared at my hands in shock, the world spinning around me.

"What the hell is going on?" I whispered to myself.

When Ava began to crawl, my teeth began to fall out. First a molar in the back. I nearly choked on it, the tooth rolling around in the back of my mouth until I leaned over and spit it out. A strand of saliva threaded with blood. A pink-washed tooth in the grass.

"Are you okay?" my husband asked, rushing over to me.

Hot pain shot through my gums like electricity, boring deep into my jaw. I poked my tongue around, feeling the empty socket. "I'm fine," I said, but my voice wavered. "I think... I need to go lie down."

Instead, I walked up to the bathroom and stared at myself in the mirror.

My face was gaunt and sunken. My aquiline nose, the dominant feature of my face, was short and straight. My hair, once thick and black, was patchy and thin. A film of blood coated my lips.

I lifted my shirt. My ribs were clearly visible in

the harsh bathroom light. My breasts were nearly nonexistent. That mole I always hated, the one right above my hip, was gone.

And my fingers were still perfectly smooth, like they were made of plastic.

My husband forced me to see the doctor.

"I'm not too concerned," he told me, after shining a light in my eyes and ordering bloodwork. "After pregnancy, your body is different. We've had a few patients who've lost teeth or hair. It's all the hormones recalibrating."

"What about my fingers?" I asked.

"They look fine to me."

He didn't even look at them closely.

"I keep losing weight," I protested.

"That's good. Most women gain weight after pregnancy."

So we left, with a promise that someone would call us when the bloodwork came in.

I wondered if my experience would have been different with a female doctor.

Unfortunately, the next doctor to call me was not mine, but Ava's.

"Is this Ava's mom?" the voice asked, on the other end of the line.

"Yes, this is Maddie," I replied.

"Maddie. Right." A pause. "This is Anna, the nurse at Bloomfield Pediatrics. We saw you on Monday, but Dr. Rodriguez told me she wants to see Ava again this week for another checkup. Is that possible?"

My heart sunk. "Why?"

"Ava's a little behind in growth," she replied, her voice chipper. "Don't worry, we're sure everything is fine. We just want to do another weigh-in, make sure she's growing fine."

"Okay," I replied, numb. I stared at Ava, chubby-cheeked and smiling, rolling a toy train across the floor.

"Is tomorrow morning good for you? We have a 10:30 am appointment..."

Her voice droned on, rattling off various appointments. I didn't hear her. My world narrowed to one thought. *Please, let there be nothing wrong. Please let her be healthy.*

"Tomorrow at 10:30 is fine," I managed to choke out.

My tongue flicked my front incisor. It was loose.

The doctor told us it was nothing to worry about. She brought Ava over to the scale with a smile. My hands wouldn't stop shaking as I sat there, powerless.

"Sixteen pounds, two ounces," she read to the nurse.

"Is that bad?" I asked.

"It's tenth percentile." She glanced at me. "Nothing to be too worried about, but we need to make sure she's getting enough food. Are you still breastfeeding?"

I shook my head.

"Okay. Can you tell me what you've been feeding her?"

I went through the foods in painstaking detail, from mashed sweet potato to pureed chicken and broth to crackers. But I couldn't stop the little voice in the back of my head, repeating the same thing, over and over.

It's not enough.

Nothing I'm doing is enough.

That night, as I rocked Ava to sleep, I fought back tears. *Please be okay,* I begged, as I stroked the back of her little head. *Please. Please gain weight and be healthy and happy.*

When the tears finally burst through, something else came with them.

My eyelashes.

Dozens of little dark crescents, stuck to my hand, shining in the glow of the night-light.

A few weeks went by. My weight dropped below a hundred pounds. Three more of my teeth fell out. Clumps of hair stuck to the drain.

My doctor was finally concerned, seeing the extra hair loss, my missing teeth. Because I wasn't just thin; I was unattractive, now, with my checkered smile and missing eyelashes.

The bloodwork came back normal, though, and continued to. More tests were ordered, and every time they came back normal. I got some referrals to specialists, but they couldn't find the cause of my health problems, either.

Ava continued to grow. She got up to the thirty-fifth percentile for her age. Every day she was smiling more, laughing more. My entire world was bright, because she *was* my world.

My husband started to grow distant. He took more and more business trips, and I suspected not all of them were strictly for business. But I didn't care anymore. Ava was flourishing, and that was all that mattered.

It was while he was gone on one of these "business trips" that Ava hit another milestone. We were sitting on the living room floor, playing with toy trains like any other day, when it happened.

"Ma ma," she said, looking up at me.

Her very first word. A rush of happiness.

I would smile, if I still had a mouth.

LAKE SERENITY

My family and I decided to take a vacation to Lake Serenity this summer. Our son likes swimming and our daughter likes boats of all kinds, so we figured it was a good choice for our family.

I actually first found out about the place through an online ad, of all things. A photo of a beautiful lake surrounded by pine trees, with scrolling white text that read *Visit Lake Serenity*. Checking out some AirBNBs in the area, we found they were a lot cheaper than the other locations we were looking at.

So we packed up the car and were on our way to upstate New York.

The AirBNB looked just like the photos: a cozy saltbox-style house on the lake, complete with a little dock to fish off of. The view of the lake was spectacular from the huge picture windows in the family room, and the house was filled with cute little tchotchkes, like signs that read "Beach This Way" and a bottle filled with seaglass. We were thrilled with the place, patting ourselves on the back for planning such an awesome vacation.

Until we saw the flyer.

In the middle of the kitchen counter, we found a handwritten note from the owner, welcoming us into her home. She also told us, however, to check out the rules on the next page. Apparently, the community was pretty strict about conduct, and vacationers had been banned from the beach before.

Curious, my wife and I flipped the page. Bold text across the top read: **Rules for Lake Serenity.** A post-it had been stuck on for good measure, asking us to read all the rules carefully.

I shrugged at my wife, and began to read.

- **Rule 1:** Boats are not allowed on the lake after dark. If you see a boat at night, or even just a light on the lake, please call the park ranger. His number is at the bottom of this page.
- **Rule 2:** There are many fish, crabs, and aquatic plants in the lake, so don't be alarmed if you feel something brush against your foot. However, if you feel

anything trying to tug you down, call for the lifeguards immediately.

- **Rule 3:** Storms are uncommon at Lake Serenity. However, in the event of one, the storm siren will go off. You must *immediately* evacuate the beach and find shelter inside when the siren sounds. Do not get into a vehicle. Do not try to go anywhere. Just find the closest dwelling and stay inside, with all doors locked, until the storm passes.
- **Rule 4:** There is an area of the lake cordoned off at the far west corner. Swimming is prohibited there. If you see someone in that section of the lake crying for help, you must ignore them. Don't worry—the lifeguards have notified the park ranger, I assure you.
- **Rule 5:** Speaking of lifeguards, there are only five lifeguards here at Lake Serenity. Their names and photos can be found on the next page. If you say see anyone else claiming to be a lifeguard, please immediately call the park ranger's office.
- **Rule 6:** One of the reasons Lake Serenity is such a popular vacation destination is that it affords beautiful views of the mountains, the forest, and the sky.

Sunsets are especially beautiful. However, if you ever see a reflection in the water that doesn't belong—for example, the reflection of a person that isn't actually there—leave the beach immediately.

- **Rule 7:** If you're out on a boat any kind, including but not limited to kayaks, canoes, paddleboats, and small row boats, be aware of a strange optical illusion that occurs in roughly the middle of the lake. If you row into this area, you will not be able to see the shoreline in any direction. If this happens, do not call for help; that will only attract unwanted attention. Instead, begin shouting "lost boat." One of the lifeguards will come out to you and guide you safely to shore. Do not try to navigate to shore by yourself.
- **Rule 8:** We have many of turtles and fish that may poke their heads above the water. However, if you ever see anything that looks larger than a turtle (roughly larger than a foot wide), please notify the lifeguards and leave the beach.
- **Rule 9:** Don't feed the ducks.

"Wow," I told my wife, Ruth. "That's a lot of rules."

I was immediately starting to regret our decision to come here—but she told me it wasn't weird. She told me private lake communities often have strict rules. The lake by her parents' house, for example, instructed people to empty their pockets of loose change before swimming. Apparently the fish would keep eating the dropped change and it was causing problems.

So I brushed it off, and we began to plan our day.

An hour later, we were driving down to the beach. Even though the house was lakefront, swimming was only allowed at a designated beach—in addition to the list of rules, there was a sign that read NO SWIMMING in our backyard, tilted askew.

Olivia and Noah ran down to the water immediately. Ruth and I followed, setting up several yards from the water. Ruth sat under the umbrella and pulled out a book. "I'm going to swim," I told her. "You sure you don't want to come with me?"

She shook her head.

So I made my way out into the water.

To be honest, I've never been that fond of lakes. There's something off-putting about the greenish-brown color, basically the color of the muck at the bottom. Whenever I swim out past where I can stand, all I can think about are snapping turtles swimming underneath me. Along with huge fish and water snakes. And long, mushy fingers of seaweed, reaching up towards my toes.

This vacation was for the kids. Not for me.

The water was cold. As soon as I stepped in, it was like little needles pricking my skin. It didn't seem to bother the kids, though—Olivia and Noah were already floating on pool noodles near the rope, arguing about how to mine diamonds in Minecraft.

I slowly waded out, further and further. The water got thicker, muddier. I couldn't see my feet at the bottom. The sun beat down on my face, hot and scorching.

I closed my eyes, held my breath—and dove underwater.

Immediately, all sound cut off. All the laughter, and splashing, and arguing—it suddenly dropped to a distant echo. It seemed quieter under the water than it should be. Like the water itself was absorbing most of the sound.

I opened my eyes underwater, but all I could see was greenish brown water.

I surfaced. Noise exploded into existence. The water dripping down my face turned ice cold. I looked around to see Olivia and Noah, still arguing near the rope, floating on their pool noodles.

I dove back under.

The sound cut off again. Distant echoes of voices. Slight vibrations of people splashing, swimming. Like simply going underwater had transported me into a different world.

Except this time, in the quiet, I heard something else.

Singing.

The sound didn't have the same quality as the distant sounds of the swimmers. It didn't seem dulled or muffled by the water. In fact, it almost sounded like someone was humming underwater—right next to me.

I surfaced, rubbing the water out of my eyes.

No one was there.

Olivia and Noah were engaged in a splash-fight, now, several yards away from me. Ruth was still reading her book on the beach. All the other people were even further away.

I was alone.

Slowly, I tilted my head so one ear went underwater. Sure enough, the singing returned. A slow, lilting melody. I frowned and pulled my ear out of the water.

Then I jumped back.

For a split second, I thought I saw something. Something under the water. Something pale and white, just floating there, next to me.

Roughly the size and shape of a person.

But there was nothing there now, except murky brown water.

"Whoa, Dad, you okay?" Noah asked.

"Yeah…" I finally tore my eyes from the water and looked at him. "Did the rules say anything about singing in the water?"

"I don't know," he said, shrugging. "Ask Mom."

I tilted my head and put my ear underwater again. This time, I didn't hear anything.

It must have just been some kid humming underwater, and somehow it transmitted really well to sound like he or she was right next to me. And what I saw, the reflections must've just confused me, and my brain filled in the details.

I made up some excuse about staying hydrated and convinced the kids to come out of the water with me for a few minutes. Then I sat next to Ruth, under the umbrella.

"I heard this weird singing, or humming, underwater. Do you remember if the rules said anything about that?"

"I don't think so," she replied. "Why would the rules say anything about that?"

"I don't know," I replied.

I shook off the feeling, and soon after, the kids and I got back in the water. Ruth finally came in with us, and the four of us floated under the bright blue sky. After a while, the incident faded from my mind. It was so nice, so beautiful, so *serene* here. I could see why they called it Lake Serenity.

We got home, ate dinner, and went to sleep

early. As I got into bed, I was convinced that we were going to have the best vacation ever.

How wrong I was.

Around 2:00 AM, I woke up to use the bathroom. On my way back, something out the window caught my eye.

There was a light, out on the water.

Like someone was out there in a boat.

Okay, that was *definitely* one of the rules. No boating after sundown. I watched the light bob gently up and down.

Then I headed downstairs and dialed the park ranger's number into my phone.

A man picked up after the third ring. "Hello?" he asked, his voice slow with sleep.

"Hi. Sorry to call you so late, but there's a boat on the lake. And these rules said I'm supposed to call you and report it."

I glanced up at the window—and my heart dropped.

The light was closer. A lot closer. Maybe only ten, twenty yards from the shore.

"It looks like the boat is coming towards our house," I told him.

And that's when the man's entire demeanor changed.

"Listen to me very carefully," he said, in a quiet voice. "Get into a room without any windows. Everyone in the house. Lock the door, and don't come out until I call you back."

"But—" I started to protest.

The phone beeped in my ear.

The call had ended.

My heart began to pound. I ran to the kids' bedroom first and woke them up, ushering them into the bathroom.

"What are you doing?" Olivia complained as she stumbled across the hallway. I told her to just stay in the bathroom with Noah while I got their mom.

I ran to Ruth, shook her awake, and led her to the bathroom too. By now, I could tell the light was incredibly close; it was shining through the curtains drawn over the bedroom windows. Just for good measure, I shielded my eyes from the windows as we walked across the hall, instructing Ruth to do the same. We made it into the bathroom, the four of us squashed in the tiny space, and I locked the door.

"What's going on?" Noah asked, clearly afraid.

"Nothing," I replied. "There's just someone out there, but the park ranger is coming. He's going to deal with it, but he told us to stay in here. Okay? Just some teenagers causing trouble, trying to rob people, or something."

As we stood there, huddled in the dark, humid bathroom, I noticed that light was coming from under the crack of the door. It was so bright—like someone was holding a spotlight up to the windows.

"Don't look at the light," I told them. Even though the rules hadn't said that, it just felt natural. There was something horribly off here.

About a minute later, the light cut out. Seconds later, my phone rang. It was the park ranger telling me that he dealt with it, that it was just some kids trying to drink out of view of their parents. "You know how it is, with teenagers in the summer; they get up to all kinds of trouble."

His voice was smooth and slick. A completely different tone than he'd had before.

I could tell he was lying.

The next morning, Ruth and I got into a fight.

"I think we should go home," I told her.

"What? Just because of those kids?"

"Yeah," I replied. "What if they break in? What if they kidnap Noah or Olivia?"

"We spent $500 on this place, Nick. It's not refundable, so, what? We're just gonna lose it all?"

"Yeah, if that means staying alive."

A dramatic eye roll and sigh from Ruth.

To give her credit, I was always anxious about safety. I was the kind of guy who checked locks five times before going to sleep. I set up security cameras around our house. Even for this vacation, I'd ruled out a few locations on account of being unsafe. Like Pine Falls, which has a huge cliff unprotected by a guardrail.

So while I was right this time, Ruth's skepticism wasn't totally out of left field.

"The kids are going to be so disappointed if we leave," Ruth finally said, her tone softening. "They're having so much fun here, and Olivia was so excited for that paddleboat ride."

We talked it over more, and eventually, I was persuaded to stay. Of course, now I wish that I hadn't listened to her. I wish I'd grabbed the kids and forced us all to go home, even if it meant them whining and moaning the entire four hour drive home.

But that morning, I had no idea the horrors that awaited us.

That afternoon, we decided to rent the paddleboat. The entire family out on the lake, in ninety-degree weather—sounds fun, doesn't it?

But Olivia really wanted to go, so I figured we might as well get it over with now.

The four of us climbed in, the boat rocking slightly in the dark water. At least it wasn't a canoe, I told myself. I couldn't stand the way those things threatened to tip at the slightest movement.

Olivia and Ruth steered us first, to the shoreline

at the opposite end of the lake. I'll admit that was kind of cool, seeing the deep forest from the water—all the little squirrels and chipmunks scurrying in the underbrush, in the cool of the shade.

We even passed the forbidden swimming area. A bright red rope cordoned off the area, and in the middle floated an orange buoy with a sign that read *NO SWIMMING*. There were two signs at the shoreline as well, faded in the sun, letters partially peeling off. Olivia giggled. "Look, Mom, it looks like that one says *O SWIMMING*, not *NO SWIMMING*."

"That's nice," Ruth replied, clearly not amused.

We paddled past our own dock, and by some long reeds that held some fish. Then, mercifully, the boat ride was over. It was time to go back to shore.

That's when everything went horribly wrong.

Noah and I were looking down at our phones as Ruth and Olivia steered us back across the lake. It was then that I heard Ruth's voice, slightly scared. "Um, how do we get back?"

I looked up—and realized I couldn't see the shoreline anymore.

Just dark, muddy water extending in every direction, reflecting the hot summer sun.

"What the hell?" I whispered.

And then I remembered the rules.

There was that one part of the lake, in the middle, with the weird optical illusion. You wouldn't be able to see the shore, the rules had said. What were we supposed to do, again? Call for the lifeguards? Call for help?

"I think we came from that way," Noah said, pointing in a random direction.

"No, it's definitely that way," Olivia replied.

"Do you have a compass?" Ruth asked me.

"Why would I just be carrying around a compass?" I replied, scowling at her.

We argued for a few minutes. The water gently lapped at the plastic sides of the paddle boat. The shore did not come into view. The kids began to panic. Olivia cupped her hands around her mouth and shouted, "Help!"

That made me remember.

"No, stop!" I shouted, grabbing her hands.

"What?" she replied.

"The rules said don't call for help," I replied. "We're supposed to shout 'lost boat.'" I cupped my hands around my mouth and shouted, as loud as I could: "HEY! LOST BOAT!"

And then motion caught my eye.

I turned to see waves in the lake. As if something was moving, just beneath the surface.

The waves were making a beeline for our boat.

"What's that?" Noah asked, his voice filled with fear.

"LOST BOAT!" I screamed, my voice echoing across the dark water. "LOST BOAT!"

The water churned. Whatever was under the

surface was only a few yards away. I grabbed Olivia and Noah's hands. Ruth did the same.

"Don't let go of my hand, okay?" I asked. "Whatever you do. Don't let go."

"Daddy," Olivia started, her voice breaking.

And then it happened.

The thing under the water collided with the side of our boat. I could see a split-second glimpse of whitish skin under the waves, and then the boat was rocking wildly back and forth, water spraying into the air. Olivia screamed. Ruth gripped the kids' hands tighter.

"LOST BOAT!" I screamed.

Crack.

The boat rocked wildly. Ruth's entire body lurched backwards. If we weren't all holding hands, she would have fallen into the water. "Lost boat!" she shouted, joining me. "Lost boat!"

Thwack.

The impact came from directly under the boat. And this time, it was too much.

The boat flipped over, and the four of us plunged into the cold water. No sound—just as before. Only cold, murky water, pressing in on all directions. I opened my eyes and looked around in the blurry darkness. Miraculously, both kids were still holding my hands. I looked up, and I could see the dark shape of the paddle boat floating above us. And another light shape, too blurry to make out.

Ruth? I thought.

Oh no, she let go.

I kicked right, tugging on my kids' hands, pulling them away from the boat. Then I kicked towards the surface. Both kids surfaced, gasping for air.

But Ruth didn't.

A soft splash sounded behind me—but it wasn't Ruth. Several yards away, a lifeguard was frantically rowing towards us in a yellow rescue raft.

"Go to the raft!" I shouted, before diving back under the water.

I had to find Ruth.

I dove under and opened my eyes, scanning the blurry, murky water. It took me only a few seconds to find her. A whitish shape among the dark water, floating motionless, slowly descending. I kicked towards her, my heart pounding.

My lungs burned, but I didn't stop until I got to her. I reached out and grabbed her arm—

It wasn't Ruth.

The skin was too loose on her wrist, shifting and sliding under my fingertips. I looked up towards the person's face, and even though everything was still so blurry, I saw there was something horribly wrong with it. Where there should have been eyes, there were just two gaping black holes, staring at me.

And it looked like it was smiling.

A blurry, grinning mouth stretching across its face.

Forgetting I was underwater, I opened my mouth and let out a scream. Bubbles erupted from my mouth, streaming towards the surface. And then something grabbed me by the arm.

No, no, no—

My head broke the surface. I coughed, I gasped, I wheezed. The lifeguard dragged me up onto the raft.

"But Ruth," I choked, "she's still down there!"

"No, she isn't."

I turned around to see Ruth at the front of the raft, her arms around both the kids. The lifeguard began to paddle frantically, kicking up water. I stared at the overturned paddleboat, slowly sinking; the dark surface of the water, reflecting the summer sun.

I didn't see any waves. Any shape swimming towards us.

After a minute, I saw the shoreline again. The noisy beach, the kids running to and fro, the teenagers splashing each other. It was like it suddenly blinked into existence. The sound, the sights, everything returning all at once.

I didn't spend any time wondering how that could be possible.

We were safe—and that's all that mattered.

We ran back to the car, cold and shaking. We

didn't say a word as I drove us back to the AirBNB. As soon as I parked the car, I turned to the three of them.

"We're leaving," I announced. "Now."

Ruth didn't fight me this time. We grabbed our stuff as quickly as we could, throwing it haphazardly into our bags and piling them up at the door. We worked quickly, silently. We all knew we had to get out of here.

But then it happened.

A droning, high-pitched sound pierced the air, rattling the windows.

The storm siren.

I ran to the window. Outside, I could see the dark stormclouds rolling in, as thick and black as night. Clustering over the lake, as if it was some sort of magnet for them.

My heart hammered in my chest. The rules were perfectly clear on this one: *stay inside.*

Do not get in a vehicle. Do not try to go anywhere. Stay inside until the storm passes.

Ruth ran over to the door, picking up our bags. "I don't care about the stupid rules. We're leaving now."

"No, we can't. We have to stay inside until the storm is over."

She stared at me for what seemed like an eternity. Then she dropped the bags and drew the deadbolt. We went around the house, double-checking that every window and door was locked. Then we huddled in the family room, in front of the big picture window that looked out over the lake.

"STORM WARNING," a mechanical voice sounded over the droning siren. "FIND SHELTER IMMEDIATELY."

Ruth squeezed my hand.

The rain started, sheets of it pelting down onto the water, turning the surface from smooth glass to a war of ripples.

So much for serenity.

The storm siren droned on for a few more seconds, the pitch eerily turning downwards, sounding like a horribly off-key song. And then there was silence, except for the rain drumming on the roof.

"Will they let us know when the storm is over? Will the siren go off again?" Olivia asked, not taking her eyes off the lake.

"I don't know," I replied. "I guess we can leave when the rain stops."

A finger of lightning shot across the sky, fracturing into a thousand pieces. I counted the seconds—six seconds later, a rumble of thunder sounded, shaking the entire house.

The lights flickered off.

"Don't panic," I told the kids, as Olivia began to whimper. In the dim light, I stumbled over to the kitchen and began pulling out drawers.

Looking for a flashlight, a candle, matches, anything. Another clap of thunder sounded, rattling the windows.

On the fourth drawer, I found a lighter. After another minute, I found a few long, fancy-looking candles and a pewter candelabra. I lit them and set it on the floor in front of us. The orange flames flickered and brightened, casting the entire place in strange shadows that shivered and shuddered.

"We just have to wait out the storm," I told them.

So the four of us sat there, staring out at the lake, watching the storm. The rain let up slightly, but then the lightning started up again with a vengeance, streaking across the sky. I sat there, holding Ruth's hand, waiting for it to pass.

And then I saw something that didn't make sense.

Next to the dock, there was a dark reflection in the water. As if someone was standing on the dock, dressed head-to-toe in black, with sickly white skin.

Except there was no one there.

The rules said something about that.

But what?

My brain was so fried with panic, I didn't remember. I got up and ran to the sheet of paper on the counter, scanning the rules. Okay. All it said was leave the beach immediately. We weren't on the beach, so we should be okay.

I sat back down on the couch, staring at the reflection.

"Something wrong?" Ruth asked.

"Do you see that?" I pointed to the reflection.

Before she could answer, it moved.

It was walking towards the shore.

Walking towards us.

We're safe. The rules just said stay off the beach, I told myself. *We're safe.*

The reflection disappeared from the water as it stepped off the dock and into our backyard.

And as it got closer, I noticed there was... a space... in the pelting rain. Something roughly human-shaped, that the rain was bouncing off, rather than going through.

"Dad...?" Noah started.

"Ssssshhhh," I replied.

The creature—the person, the ghost, whatever it was—stood outside the window for several minutes. When the rain let up, it was nearly invisible; but as soon as it began to pelt down again, I could see it clearly. When lightning flashed across the sky, I could almost see the contours of its pale face, its black dress rippling in the wind, its long hair wet and matted against its shoulders.

I told myself it was just my imagination.

But I knew it wasn't.

After several more minutes, I couldn't take it. Sitting here, watching this *thing* stand in the rain, watching us. I got up and began to pace the room. I checked my phone—no service. I forced myself not to look at the window, and instead focused on the tiniest details of the cabin. Like the knots in the wood that seemed to look like faces. The fake succulent on the coffee table. The "Beach This Way" sign, which seemed more of a threat now. The books on the shelf against the wall.

Then I stopped. There was one book that stuck out like a sore thumb—it was much, much older than the others. Cloth, teal cover, with gold-embossed lettering on the spine read THE HISTORY OF LAKE SERENITY.

I pulled it out and flipped it open. My heart dropped as I scanned the first page.

In total, 32 people have gone missing at Lake Serenity since 1900. Despite the lake being dredged several times, no bodies have ever been found. Those more inclined to the supernatural believe the lake is 'cursed'...

I flipped the page.

There was a photo of a pale woman in a long, fluttery black dress, with the caption: *Young widow drowned, 1918. Suspected murder; killer never found.*

Next page.

Three men, in a small motorboat, lost in storm. 1962.

Next page—

"Dad?" Olivia asked, her voice shaking.

I looked up.

And all the blood drained out of my face.

Ruth.

No, no, no...

Ruth's eyes were sunken back into her eye sockets, hidden in deep shadow. Her skin was a sickly white, drooping and hanging off her face like it was too loose for her skull.

She looked like the creature I saw in the lake.

Not blurry, this time.

As the candlelight flickered over her face, all traces of Ruth faded away. Her eyes sunk further back until I couldn't see them anymore. Just empty pits of darkness, staring at me. Her mouth widened into a smile, revealing rows of needle-like piranha teeth.

"Run!" I screamed, lunging to Noah and Olivia and grabbing them by the arms.

The creature made a guttural gasping sound. Then, with a wet *slap,* it fell on its hands and knees to the floor. It made its way towards us, grinning all the while, empty eye sockets staring up at us.

I scrambled to unlock the deadbolt.

The storm wasn't over, but as soon as the door was open, we ran.

We made it to the car. Doors slammed. Engine revved. I pulled out onto the road, kicking up gravel as I hit the gas.

Olivia and Noah sobbed in the backseat. I kept

my eyes on the road, numb, my only focus to get my kids safely out of Lake Serenity as soon as possible.

And that's my story. My wife, Ruth, was the 33rd life claimed by Lake Serenity.

So, if you ever see an ad for a beautiful lake among deep wilderness, promising amazing sunsets and fun for the whole family... don't go. I beg you, don't go.

The lake has claimed enough victims.

OUIJA BOARD

Today was a good day for talking to the dead.

That's the thought I woke up with when I saw it was one of those gray, rainy days. Days where I felt my loneliness harder than ever. People walked by on the sidewalk, in twos and threes, their forms blurred by the pouring rain. *Drip, drip, drip.*

I went up to the attic and grabbed the dusty old Ouija board. I hadn't used it in years. I set the board on the coffee table and grabbed the planchette, taking in a deep breath.

Does this work with just one person?

I gently placed my middle and index finger on the planchette, positioning it over the G to start. I took a deep breath in, let it out.

"Spirits, we call to you."

For a moment, nothing happened.

And then the planchette began to move. I watched in horror as my fingers moved over the letters:

I-S-A-N-Y-O-N-E-T-H-E-R-E

"Y-yes?" I said, my voice a little hoarse.

W-H-A-T-I-S-Y-O-U-R-N-A-M-E

My throat tightened. Why did the spirit want to know my name? "Ada," I replied, my voice wavering.

A-R-E-Y-O-U-H-A-P-P-Y-A-D-A

Cold chills ran down the entire length of my body. I closed my eyes tight. "Yes," I finally said. "I suppose I'm happy enough." I took a deep breath in, a deep breath out. That wasn't really true—but it was the simplest answer I could give.

I opened my eyes.

There wasn't just one hand on the planchette. There were *two*.

I leapt back and shrieked. In an instant, the hand was gone. I sat there, panting, my heart going a mile a minute.

Shaking, I made my way back to the Oujia board. Placed my fingers on the planchette. "Who are you?"

The planchette moved under my hands almost frantically, snapping from letter to letter.

H-O-W

D-I-D

Y-O-U...

My throat went dry as it spelled out the final word.

D-I-E

What the hell?

What kind of mind games was this spirit trying to play?

The planchette moved again.

W-H-O

K-I-L-L-E-D

Y-O-U

"I'm not dead!" I shrieked. "*You are!*"

The planchette was deathly still under my fingers.

"STOP! *STOP IT!!!*"

But then something flashed through my brain.

Alone. I was alone because I'd moved out. A rainy day like this one. I'd made it to a friend's house, but he'd had followed me, didn't he?

It was *his* form standing in the doorway as the rain pattered on the tin roof. It was water dripping off *his* face that I heard plopping to the floor.

Drip, drip, drip.

"M—" I started, saying his name.

But it was too late.

The planchette careened from under my fingers, settling on **GOOD-BYE.**

And then there was silence.

I was sitting in the house, all alone, on an endless rainy day.

Silhouettes flit by on the sidewalk, blurred through the windows, without faces or form. The silence was only broken by the sound of the rain.

Drip, drip, drip.

STAY ALERT: CHILDREN WALKING ON ROADWAY

That was the sign I saw when I turned onto old Country Ave.
STAY ALERT
Children Walking on Roadway
It was accompanied by the silhouette of a child kicking a ball. I paused for a second, staring at the sign. *Isn't it usually SLOW: Children At Play?*

The sign was old, the fluorescent yellow paint cracking around the edges. There weren't many houses on Country Ave. anymore, not since the town had condemned several of the structures. Flattened piles of rubble were all that were left. I hadn't been on the road in years, but that's what I heard from Jackie. Were there still actually children playing on this road?

I walked up the hill, my heart pumping, my legs aching. Usually I wouldn't take my morning walk on this road, but I wanted to take an extra-long walk to compensate for all the cake last night. Country Road went straight up a hill, at a 30 or 40-degree angle, and wove around the trees and boulders like a drunk snake.

I crested the hill—and that's when I saw the next sign.

STAY ALERT

Do Not Speak To Children

I stopped, frowning at the sign. Um, okay? Was that because of a kidnapping incident or something? Or possibly children with cognitive difficulties or social anxiety? I stared at the silhouette drawing under the warning. It was an adult with their hands over their mouth.

Weird.

I continued walking. The road had flattened out a bit, now, and one of the razed structures was on my right. Just a gap in the trees, now, with some wooden slabs and chunks of concrete on the forest floor.

In a few months, I bet you wouldn't even be able to tell a structure was there, as the crawling vines and brambles engulfed it.

I went around another crook in the road—and there was another sign.

This one was different. It was white, with no drawings—just text. And it looked new. It wasn't peeling and dirty like the other signs, and I noticed fresh dirt along the bottom, as if it had just been erected days ago.

The text it held, however, was terrifying.

IF YOU TRAVEL BEYOND THIS POINT, YOU ARE RESPONSIBLE FOR THE COST OF YOUR SEARCH AND RESCUE

There was nothing immediately dangerous beyond the sign. Just the road, which had straightened out, cutting through the forest. And one more sign, several yards ahead—a standard **SLOW: Children Crossing** sign. Like the type they put up around schools.

Is it dangerous because of all the construction?

Maybe they put it up when they were demolishing all the houses...

Either way, I wasn't going to screw around with the law. I turned around, to head back—

And my breath caught in my throat.

There was a child behind me. Peeking out from around a tree. As soon as I turned, she was already darting out of sight.

My heart dropped.

What... the fuck?

I almost called out a hello—just to announce my presence, to maybe scare her—but then I remembered the sign. *Do not speak to children.* I took a deep breath and started walking back down the road, towards home. It meant I would pass the kid, but I had to get out of here somehow.

Snap.

I whipped around.

No.

Several yards behind me, at the *children crossing* sign, there was a line of children. They stood in the street, holding hands, stretching across the entire width of the street. Boys and girls, maybe eight or so. Wearing old-style clothing, jumpers and dresses, overalls and button-down shirts.

What the...?

I have to get out of here.

I picked up my pace. I could see the little girl's hands poking around the trunk to my left. She was still hiding there. *Waiting for me?*

I picked up the pace.

Her fingers... they were so pale. Grayish. Wrinkled and pruny like she'd spent too much time in the bath or at the pool.

Fuck this.

I broke into a sprint.

I could hear voices singing behind me. Children's voices. Singing *row, row, row your boat* but too slow, slightly off key. The tree approached—I kept my eyes on the road—

But I could see her in the corner of my eye.

There was something *horribly* wrong with her face.

Her eyes were dark, empty pits. Her mouth was stretched into a wide, open grin, revealing pointed, needle-like teeth. Her skin was grayish green, her dress frayed and faded—

I broke into a faster run. My feet slapped painfully on the pavement. Running downhill, I felt like I might suddenly trip and fly down the rest of the hill. Every step felt off-balance. But eventually I was at the bottom, at Main Street. I ran onto the sidewalk and stopped, gasping for breath.

A passerby asked me if I was okay.

"Don't... don't go on that road," I choked out, pointing behind me.

Eventually, I had the courage to turn around. For a moment, I saw the tip of a red sneaker poking out from behind the tree next to the sign for Country Rd.

Then it was gone.

And I was, thankfully, alone.

A THOUSAND DEATHS

I died for the first time when I was twelve years old.

Asthma attack. Huffing and wheezing. Throat closing like invisible fingers were crushing my windpipe. By the time I made it into the ER, I was legally dead.

But just two minutes later, before the doctors even had time to tell my family—my eyes shot open and I came back to life.

The next time it happened, I was seventeen. My car, wrapped around a tree, after coming home from a party. I wasn't drunk, but I was tired, and the roads in this part of the country twist and curve over the mountains like hands caressing a lover. I saw the guardrail half a second too late.

Declared dead at the scene.

Until I sat up and walked away, nearly giving the EMT a heart attack.

At my first job after college, I stepped into a faulty elevator. The cable snapped and the elevator fell seven stories. I should've been pulverized.

But I survived.

By this point, I knew there was something different about me. It wasn't even like I was cheating death—death seemed to be *finding* me. How many people have had three near-fatal accidents before they turn 25?

Other people began to notice, too. I was interviewed on TV a few times. Searching my name online brought up a slew of message board posts and YouTube videos, all discussing me.

"Do you see anything, when you're dead?" the reporter had asked me, in my interview with WN94.

"You mean, like a near death experience?" I asked.

She nodded, grinning wide with anticipation.

"No. I don't see anything," I replied. "Or if I did, I don't remember."

But that was a lie.

Every time I died, I remembered what happened. First: black, undulating, shimmering stars. Then numbness, spreading throughout my whole body. My soul, folding in on itself over and over again. A black hole, a singularity, taking up only a single point the size of a dust speck, in the middle of my brain.

And then, I saw it.

Not a light at the end of the tunnel.

Two lights.

Two eyes, staring intently down at me. Connected to a face in shadow. It didn't move, didn't speak. Just stared at me with eyes that shone wetly in the darkness.

And then I'd wake up.

As years went by, the frequency of my deaths increased—and so did the amount of time I stayed dead. Last year, after falling into a sewer, I'd woken up in the morgue. Surrounded by sheet-covered bodies. It no longer felt like I was having near-death experiences; it felt like I was being followed.

No, *pursued*.

The entity with the eyes like stars, skin like a thousand galaxies twisting and turning on each other, was the predator. I was the prey.

Maybe it let me go for the fun of it.

A game of cat and mouse.

The next time I died, I was thirty-seven. I was doing dishes in my apartment when a stray bullet hit me in the chest. As red soaked my shirt, I caught my reflection in the window above the sink.

The entity was standing behind me.

A dark shadow, long arms twisting around my waist, with skin that rippled and moved in a way my brain couldn't quite process. I tried to stare, but the stars fluttered over my vision, blocking it out...

my soul coiled in on itself, smaller, smaller, a dust speck in the vast universe...

I saw it. Hovering over me, moving and writhing and shimmering. Eyes focused on me, staring into my infinitesimal soul.

This time, for the first time, I spoke.

"What do you want?"

The creature shifted, starry eyes focusing on me. Fear roiled through me—or what was left of me. It could hear me.

"Why do you keep following me? Why do you keep *killing* me?"

A pause.

I am not killing you, child.

A voice that sounded like a chorus of many voices, vibrating through my tiny speck of a soul. I was frozen, suspended, in the void.

I am protecting you from death.

The entity shifted. Beyond it stood a figure, tall and gaunt, with limbs stretching nearly to the floor. It advanced slowly towards us, slow methodical footsteps through the nothing.

It is not your time yet, child.

My eyes flew open.

I was lying on the floor of my apartment, covered in blood. I forced myself up; pain ran down my arm, electric and hot. I fumbled for the phone and dialed 911, every heartbeat sending a fresh wave of pain through my body.

As I sat there, waiting, the words of the entity replayed in my mind.

I realized something.

My first death, when I was twelve... was the only death due to natural causes. Every other time had been an accident.

Had death been pulling at the strings of fate, tipping the scales of cosmic probability, in favor of my demise? And the entity, with the starry eyes and rippling skin, had been saving me?

It is not your time yet, child.

Sirens pierced the air, growing closer with every second.

I lay back down, closed my eyes, and waited.

I'M AN ANIMAL CONTROL OFFICER

I started working as an animal control officer in Oak Valley, Pennsylvania last month. It's a little town just south of the Pocono mountains, surrounded on all sides by deep forest. And even though I've worked in the animal control field for several years now, there is something horribly *off* about the animals here in Oak Valley.

To be fair, they warned me. During my orientation, they told me that Oak Valley was a little different. That it had a much more diverse ecosystem than most places. That there were many animals here I may have never seen before. They gave me a handbook, even, of common flora and fauna—that is, plants and animals—I was likely to encounter. I was supposed to read it, but I was so busy moving into my apartment, I didn't open it once.

I guess that means everything that happened is my fault.

Let me start from the beginning. One of my first calls, on my second day of work, was from a woman named Nancy Delaney. She told me a bat had gotten stuck in her wall. She'd heard high-pitched chittering sounds all night, along with frantic scratching and scrambling sounds. "I think it's stuck in there and I don't know what to do," she told me. "Poor thing sounds panicked."

It was late, near midnight, and I was the only one on duty. So I set out to her house alone. It really should've been a routine call; I've had dozens of these before. Usually, we coax the bat towards the outside of the house with noise and lights. As a last resort, we cut a hole in the drywall and pull it out. Wearing thick leather gloves, of course, so I don't get bitten.

When I pulled up to the house, though, it was completely dark. Not a single light on. A sprawling old Victorian, dark and silent as death. I thought maybe I had the wrong address—she knew I was coming, wouldn't she turn on a light for me? But when I checked, it was the right house.

I got my gear, walked up the steps, and knocked.

A woman immediately answered the door. She was so quick, she must've been waiting right on the other side of the door for me. Which was weird. I brushed it off and began to introduce myself, but she interrupted me. "Be quiet," she whispered. "Or it'll hear you."

A chill went down my spine.

The way she said it... she was *terrified*. Which, in turn, made *me* terrified. Generally speaking, I'm not scared of the animals; I'm scared of rabies, which is one of the most horrible ways to die. But she seemed so scared, it rubbed off on me.

She quietly ushered me inside and pointed at the stairs. An old, narrow, rickety staircase that led up to a pitch-black second floor.

"It's up there," she whispered. "In the wall of our bedroom."

I started going up the stairs—but she didn't follow.

"Do you want to show me exactly where you heard it?" I asked.

She shook her head.

Okay, well, that's weird, I thought as I ascended. On the second floor, there were a few doors, but I quickly found her bedroom. It was the only one not decked out with cartoon characters and Disney princesses.

Where are her kids, anyway? I thought. *Are they over a friend's house or something?*

The whole thing was giving me the creeps. I sent a quick text to my girlfriend, letting her know where I was, and telling her to call me if I didn't get back to her in an hour. Then I set out my equipment and began my process.

I try not to rush things with animal removal. There's an art to it, sort of. If you're willing to cooperate, and let the animals take the lead, you'll find yourself better off. *Go with nature, not against it,* was something my old boss said all the time. And he was right. Unless you were dealing with a rabid or aggressive animal, or someone's safety was threatened, it was always better to step aside and let the animal take the lead.

So I stood in the middle of the room for several minutes, just listening.

For a long time, I didn't hear anything. Just pure silence. But then—from the wall to my left—I heard it. A series of scratching noises, followed by a soft scrambling sound, like wings against drywall. A sound I was all too familiar with.

I approached the wall. The scrambling sounds got louder, as it felt the vibrations of my footsteps. I went slow. Again, no reason to make the bat panic. When I got to the wall, I waited, breathing slow.

Then I started trying to coax it outside. I softly hit the wall, again and again, in a motion towards the outside. Hopefully, the bat would move away from the sound. I only had about a twenty-five percent success rate with this method, but it was so low effort it was worth trying. A lot better than just cutting a hole in the wall.

I continued tapping the wall.

For a minute, there was just silence. Then the scratching sounds resumed—but they were in a different place. A few feet above my head, almost where the wall met the ceiling. Okay, that was good—the bat was moving. It hadn't flown in quite the right direction, but progress was progress.

I continued hitting the wall—when I heard another scratching sound.

Coming from the opposite wall.

Oh, no. There's a second one.

I walked out of the room, to the top of the stairs, and called down to the woman: "How many bats did you say you heard?"

Silence.

"Hello? Are you down there?"

Nothing.

Shaking my head, I went back into the room.

But things had gotten worse. Much worse.

There were more scrambling sounds. Coming from every direction. Every wall. Oh no. We were dealing with an *infestation* here. Not just a single bat.

Why didn't she tell me that?

And then the chittering began. Shrill. High-pitched. Frantic.

Not all people can hear bats chitter. It's at a very high frequency, and the older you get, the less likely you'll be able to hear it. But I could always hear it—and this was the first time I regretted that ability. It was so loud. Screeching, shrill, panicked. Coming from every direction. I resisted the urge to cover my ears.

How many of them are there?

I started to panic. This was bad—really bad. I wasn't equipped to deal with a colony of bats. Why didn't the woman just say that? Why did she pretend like it was just one that I just needed to cut out and rescue? Was she hoping I'd get rid of all of them, and save her an exterminator bill?

The chittering screeched in my ears.

But I didn't leave. However many bats were in there, they did *not* sound happy. It was my duty to give it another try. Maybe if I could scare one bat out, the rest would follow it. I started banging on all the walls, fanning out towards the window.

The chittering got louder.

Like it was agitating them.

One more try. I sucked in a breath and banged the walls, harder this time, walking towards the window.

And that's when I noticed something I hadn't before.

There was a little hole in the wall. About an inch in diameter, at knee height.

Perfect.

Bats generally move away from light. This was

my chance. I crouched down and turned on the flashlight on my phone.

Then I brought it up to the hole.

I immediately jumped back.

Not because I saw a bat.

Because I saw an *eye,* staring back out at me.

I didn't even get my stuff. I just ran. Ran down the rickety stairs as the chittering reached a fever pitch, echoing throughout the house.

Because the eye was too big to be a bat's. *Way* too big. And the eye was shaped like a *human's*... not totally round, like an animal's.

It matched no creature I'd ever seen.

As I pulled out of the driveway, I noticed the garage door was open. No cars inside.

The woman had fled, too. She'd abandoned me in the house, and left me to deal with... whatever this thing was. Alone.

I drove right back to the facility and called my boss. He didn't seem surprised by what I was saying—he just told me to write up a full report, and to leave not a single detail out, no matter how strange it sounded.

He also told me he'd handle this case for the time being.

I ended my shift in a daze, drove home, and collapsed on the bed.

After that, I started noticing how odd the other cases were.

We got a call about a bear tearing up someone's screen door. But the tracks in the mud looked too big to be a bear's. Almost two feet across, with claws about four inches long. At the time, I'd chalked it up to the mud being too soft. But now, I wasn't so sure.

Maybe it wasn't a bear at all.

And then there was the fox. During my second week in Oak Valley, someone had reported a mangy looking fox at the edge of their property. The animal we took in, however, was too large to be a fox—and too small to be a coyote. Even with all my expertise, I couldn't quite place what it was. Some sort of coyowolf hybrid? Just a really large fox? It also acted strange—it didn't seem to be afraid of us at all, and would just stare at us for hours from its crate. We sent it away to the state animal control facility, but never heard an update.

And the opossum someone called in a few nights ago was strange too. If you've ever seen one, you know that they're notoriously slow. That's why they unfortunately get run over so often. But this one was incredibly fast, scampering up a tree before we could even get our equipment out.

If it weren't for the thing in the wall, I would've just brushed all these things off. But everything together was too much.

I decided to ask my coworker, Jack. He was an older man in his 50s, with a grizzled white beard and a pair of gold-rimmed glasses. Didn't take any BS from anyone. He usually worked the day shift, but I caught him before he left, and told him what I'd seen in the wall.

He didn't seem the least bit concerned. "Sounds like a parasite," he told me, as he packed up his stuff.

"A parasite? Aren't those usually bugs and worms and stuff?"

"Not *that* kind of parasite, Benjamin," he replied. "The kind that latch on to a person's negative energy. Sounds like Mrs. Delaney was carrying around some emotional baggage. We often find them in bedrooms, where all the energy is, 'cause they're tossing and turning all night. Pretty common around these parts. Anyway, I'm going to head out. Need anything else?" he asked.

"No," I replied.

What the hell was he talking about? A parasite of someone's energy? I shook my head. But then again—what I'd seen didn't make any sense. I'd never seen anything like it, in my almost decade of work as an animal control officer. The eye was large, completely black, and shaped like a human's. I would think the creature attached to it would be too big to fit inside the wall, unless its eyes were strangely disproportionate to the rest of its body.

And it didn't match anything I'd ever trapped or studied during training. Ever.

The rest of my shift went smoothly. I got a call about a raccoon ripping open someone's trash, and was relieved to find a completely normal-looking raccoon. However, only an hour before my shift ended—just before six am—things took a turn for the worst.

I got a call about a deer in someone's yard.

Now, listen, Oak Valley is overrun with deer. They're everywhere—in backyards, on the roads, *everywhere*. You can't drive five miles without seeing one. So I wasn't sure why this guy was calling about a deer in his backyard.

Until he described it.

"I think it might have chronic wasting disease or something. It's really thin, and it's drooling. It doesn't seem to be afraid of me, either. It's just been standing there for like, an hour."

"An hour?" I asked.

"Yeah. I would think it's dead or something, but every so often it twitches. It's really weird," he replied.

I told him we'd be on our way and that he shouldn't go outside until we dealt with it. But right before he hung up, he told me something else.

"Its eyes... I don't know how to describe it. But there's too much white in its eyes. Almost like... they're *human* eyes... on a deer."

Well, that wasn't creepy at all.

I drove to his house and, sure enough, there was the deer. It stood near the treeline, perfectly still, staring at us. A thin line of drool dripping from its mouth, glistening in the morning sun.

It looked like a textbook case of chronic wasting disease. That's the disease people call "zombie deer disease," and it fit the bill: it was thin, and a hoard of flies buzzed around it. Its ears drooped. And it didn't even flinch when I slammed the van doors.

Yikes. I hadn't dealt with one of these for five years. I forgot how... unsettling they were. It stared at me as I went around the back of the van and got my clover trap out. By law, we have to trap and test any deer suspected of having chronic wasting disease, unfortunately.

As I got closer to the deer, however, I saw that the guy was right. There was something horribly wrong with the deer's eyes. They *did* almost look human. They were the right shape for a deer, but there was way too much sclera, the white part. And the eyes themselves were set more on the front of the deer's head, so it could look straight ahead—like a predator.

It stared at me as I approached.

Some weird breed of deer? Some sort of mutation? I wondered. I walked around it with a wide berth, aiming to set the trap up between it and the forest. I immediately felt relief as soon as I got behind it, and it wasn't staring at me anymore.

I set up the trap up ten yards behind the deer. Now it was time to wait. I told the guy to stay inside the house, not to let anyone out, and to call the office when the deer was finally trapped.

As I headed back to the van, the hair on the back of my neck prickled. I turned around to see the deer still staring at me. Its eyes were actually following my movement, even though it remained perfectly still.

A chill went down my spine.

I got back to the facility, and when Jack came in for his shift, I told him to expect a call about the deer. Then I drove back home and promptly fell asleep.

When I got back the next evening, however, Jack was waiting for me with a grim look on his face. "Why didn't you tell them to keep their pets inside?" he demanded.

I stood there, confused. "What?" I asked.

"The deer. It mauled their cat. It's okay, but it's gonna be a hefty vet bill, and an extra round of vaccines."

What? It attacked their cat? I stood there, frozen. Deer with chronic wasting disease weren't that aggressive, or even capable of hurting pets. Were they? It had been a while since I reviewed the facts.

But the one I'd dealt with years ago wasn't aggressive.

"I don't understand. Deer don't attack pets," I told Jack.

"Just tell me next time, okay? I need to know what we're dealing with, here." Then he walked away to start packing up, without offering any further explanation.

There's something horribly wrong here.

The bat thing. The deer. All the other weird animals I'd seen. So, as soon as Jack left, I went to the computer to check some of the log books. They kept a record of every call, every creature captured. Maybe something in there would tell me what was going on.

I pulled up some of the files from the past few months, before I got here. There were lots of entries for rabid-looking opossums, raccoons getting into people's garbage, et cetera. But then I noticed an entry for March of this year.

Under "type of animal," someone had just typed "UNKNOWN."

Under "incident description," it said the following:

Caller described biped animal pacing around cabin. Growls and clicking sounds heard. Officer on scene described frantic clicking sounds but did not catch sight of creature. No one was harmed. No other details given. Status: closed.

Another entry from April listed the creature as 'UNKNOWN,' and the incident report read:

Caller claimed that she heard a baby crying in the woods. Called police; police found no baby. Caller continued hearing the crying late into the night. Around 4 AM, caller saw what she described as 'a skinny person running on all fours across the back of her yard.' She was the only witness. May be related to case number 3401. Status: open.

A chill went down my spine.

And then I remembered the manual that my boss, Frank, had given me during orientation. When I got home, I pulled it out and flipped through the pages. And then I saw it; beyond chapters that explained rabies protocol and how to identify different canines, there was a chapter simply titled 'Ongoing Investigations.'

And what lay in there shocked me.

There were pictures of animals that didn't exist. Rabbit-looking animals with two heads and red eyes. Snakes intertwined and melded together. Things with oozing skin, black eyes, tentacle-like appendages that dangled across the pages.

And in there, I saw the creatures I'd seen, too. A carnivorous deer with human-like eyes. A wrinkly, thin creature with enormous black eyes—and papery skin stretched across its arms, that reminded me of bat's wings. Scanning the description, I saw the word *parasite* over and over.

So it was all true.

All the creatures existed.

Here, tucked away in the Pocono mountains, were strange, deadly cryptids no one had ever heard of.

That all brings me to the call I got last night. Which was, by far, the worst.

If only I'd done more. I'd read the manual for hours, but I still wasn't prepared. There's no way I could have been prepared for the horrors that awaited me at 79 Valley Road.

The old man called me a little after 1 AM. He sounded terrified. "Please. There's something in my backyard."

"Can you describe what it is?" I asked him. "Does it seem big, like a bear, or small like a raccoon?"

"I don't know," he whispered into the phone. "It's just making these horrible gurgling sounds. It sounds like it's dying or something. I don't know."

It took me nearly fifteen minutes to get there. He was right on the edge of town; his property bordered the State Park, with hundreds of acres of wilderness and hiking trails. I shuddered picturing all the things I'd seen in the manual, crawling and creeping and flying out of those woods.

I got out of the van and walked up to his house.

The old man didn't look well. His hands trembled as he led me in. "It's right outside," he whispered. "Out back."

I walked through the house and over to the sliding glass door. The man didn't come with me; he just stood in the kitchen, poking his head around the corner, watching me.

"It's there. Right out there," he whispered, pointing.

I looked out the door into the darkness. Nothing. I pulled out my flashlight and swept it across the yard through the glass. Still nothing. I glanced back at the old man, my stomach twisting. *Maybe he has trouble with his mind. Maybe he just thought he saw something.*

I wish, desperately, that were the case.

"Look in the trees," the old man said.

That sentence sent a shiver down my spine. I tilted my flashlight up, at the single oak tree in the middle of his backyard.

I froze.

There was something sitting in the tree. From my vantage point, I couldn't tell exactly how big it was. But its eyes reflected in the flashlight's light perfectly. It was sitting ten feet off the ground, just staring at us.

I opened the sliding glass door a crack and shouted a "HEY!" If it was a bear, or any other *normal* wild animal, it would run. This creature, however, didn't. It just kept staring down at us from the tree, eyes glowing.

So it wasn't a normal wild animal, then.

It was something from the manual.

I closed and locked the sliding glass door. Pulled the manual out of my bag and flipped through it. There were some creatures I could rule out right away—like the two-headed rabbit thing. But knowing it was large and able to climb trees didn't narrow down the search *that* much. There was a huge, bear-like creature with fangs the size of a sabertooth tiger's. And a tall, humanoid dryad-looking thing that sat in trees and lured unsuspecting people to their deaths. I flipped back and forth through the pages, then turned to the old man.

"You said it was making a sort of guttural sound?"

"It was at first," the old man replied, "but now it almost sounds like it's... talking. I know that sounds crazy, but I thought I could hear it whispering actual words. Well, just one word. A name." His voice dropped to just barely above a whisper. "It said *my* name."

"What?"

"My wife died a year ago. Maybe it's just my mind playing tricks on me, but I could have sworn that thing said my name—in her voice."

I turned back to the door, shining my flashlight up into the tree. And every muscle in my body froze.

The creature was gone.

"Close all the windows and lock the doors," I shouted. The two of us frantically ran through the house.

Then I called both Frank and Jack. Neither answered. So I sat down with him in the kitchen and tried to get more details out of him. He didn't have much. He only kept telling me that the thing was calling for him, in his dead wife's voice.

"I think it's trying to lure me out there," he told me. "It wants me to leave the house."

"Well, you're not going to."

We were safe inside here. At least, I thought we were. Nothing I read about any of the creatures in the manual made me think they could break down doors. We would just have to wait it out. I tried calling Frank and Jack again. No answer.

And then, about twenty minutes later, I heard the floorboards creaking above us.

No. No, it can't be, I told myself. "Everything was closed up, right?" I asked the old man.

He looked back at me fearfully.

"One of the windows in my bedroom was open. I closed it, but maybe... maybe it got in before I closed it."

I stared at him. *Why didn't he tell me that?*

More sounds came from above us. Light, flitting footsteps.

As if the creature were *skipping* across the hallway upstairs.

I grabbed my stun gun out of my bag. I told the old man to call the police and stay downstairs. Then I started upstairs, aiming the gun ahead of me.

I wish I remembered all the creatures in the manual. But there were so many of them. Dozens... At least I remember reading that our stun guns had higher doses of tranquilizer, to be effective against *all* creatures. Whatever this was, as long as I shot at it, we'd be fine.

And then I realized what it was. *The dryad thing. It lures people. With a human voice.* I crept up the stairs, listening to the footsteps, trying to pinpoint the source.

They were coming from the room ahead of me, at the end of the hallway.

I swallowed, my throat dry, and stalked towards the door.

That's when I heard it. A voice. No—my *girlfriend's* voice—calling out to me.

"Benjamin."

I raised the stun gun, my hands shaking.

I think the creature must have sensed my hesitation, because its cries suddenly grew desperate. It began to cry. Plead with me. "Please help me," it called. "It hurts. It hurts so much."

My heart broke listening to it. *It isn't real,* I told myself, as I stepped closer to the door. *It isn't real.*

Then I reached down and twisted the doorknob. Hand on the trigger, I pushed the door open and stepped into the room.

Nothing could have prepared me for what I saw inside.

It looked like a woman—sort of. Its skin was rough bark, and its hair was made of dry, dead leaves. Its eyes were the most human thing about it, pupils the color of dark rotting soil, locked on me. Mythology paints dryads as beautiful, but this creature was made of death, made of the decaying forest floor.

Its head, if you could call it that, bobbed on its neck as it took a step forward.

I pulled the trigger.

In an instant, the dryad darted into the shadows. I fired a few more shots blindly, but I didn't hit the creature—because I heard the shattering of glass, and then it was disappearing into the woods.

Perfectly camouflaged among the trees.

When the police arrived, they swept the property. But they didn't find any evidence of the creature. I helped the old man move into a motel room for the night. He assured me he wouldn't open the door for anyone, and that he would be perfectly safe.

He wasn't.

The next morning, I got a call from the deputy. The old man had been found dead, sitting by the window. The autopsy hadn't been done yet, but it was suspected to be a heart attack.

The news was a shock to me. I blamed myself. If I had only made the shot, maybe he would still be alive. There was no doubt in my mind that the dryad killed him. No matter how natural the death looked.

I sat down with Frank the next day and asked him to tell me everything about Oak Valley.

I was paying full attention, this time.

"There's something different about Oak Valley, as you've probably already guessed," he said. "There are beings here... beyond our understanding. We try to keep the residents safe, but it's a delicate balance. We don't want to risk enraging the creatures, either—some of them can be quite vengeful."

"What are they?"

Frank spoke for a long time, but he explained to me that Oak Valley was near a fault line of sorts. Somewhere deep in the Pocono Mountains. All the creatures came from it. Some of them never left the woods, but others made their way into our town. Frank and his crew would always try to deal with them the best they could, and stop them from escaping to the rest of the world. He told me that, just like normal animals, most of them don't *want* to attack humans. But some were actively malicious, actively evil, like the dryad I'd encountered.

"If I'd just made the shot, he'd still be alive," I told Frank.

"We can't get them all," he said sadly.

Later that day, we got another call from Nancy Delaney. About the thing in her walls. It had, apparently, gotten out.

"You feeling up to it, or should I let Jack handle this one?" Frank asked.

I thought for a moment.

"I'll take it," I told him.

Then I packed up my things and headed out in the van, towards the Victorian house at the edge of town.

WHITE NOISE, BLACK SCREEN

There is a video on YouTube simply titled "White Noise, Black Screen." It is a 10-hour-long video, designed for playing while you're asleep.

It stands out among the other white noise videos though, because at around the 6-hour mark, there is a huge spike in the "most replayed" section.

In case you don't know—"most replayed" is a feature on YouTube that shows what part of the video other people played over and over again. For most videos, it makes sense—on a creepy urban explorers video, the "most replayed" might be where the person encounters a ghost or creepy person, etc. Or a funny skit video might be most replayed at the punchline.

But for a video that's playing white noise and a black screen for 10 hours, why would there be a most replayed section?

But there it was. A 30-second portion of the video at the timestamp 6 hours, 18 minutes.

Out of curiosity, I jumped to that part of the video and played it. But it looked and sounded the same as the rest of the video: black screen, white noise. No blips in the audio or change to the visuals, as far as I could tell.

Maybe that's when most people get up. I mean, that was six hours of sleep, right? Maybe a lot of people woke up about 6 hours into the video and shut it off.

That wouldn't really be replaying it, though.

And also, 30-seconds in a 10 hour video was too accurate. Some people would wake up six hours in, six hours five minutes in... etc. The "most replayed" feature showed a spike at exactly 6:18:14. A huge, narrow spike—specifically at that time—not a broader hump that would imply a range of wakeup times.

Maybe someone linked the video at that time by accident, and shared it to a lot of people?

Comments were turned off, so I couldn't check if people were saying anything else about it.

Despite the weirdness, that night, I decided to play the video while I slept. That's how I found the video in the first place—I really did need white noise. My neighbor's dog kept barking at 6 AM and I needed sleep.

I pressed PLAY on the video and went to bed.

And woke up with a start in the middle of the night.

I didn't know what woke me up. My phone said it was 3:37 AM. My room was pitch black, except for the dark-gray glow of the "White Noise, Black Screen" video playing. I rolled over, pulled the blanket over me, and tried to fall back asleep.

But my body was pumping with adrenaline. It was like I'd woken up from a nightmare or something, even though I didn't remember having one. I tried to relax, slowly counting in my head.

That's when I heard something else.

It's hard to describe, but I'll try. Some white noises are computer-generated, so that they truly make a uniform rushing sound the entire time. Others, however, especially in older "sound machines" are actually a clip of white noise repeating over and over again. Listening to it long enough, your brain starts to pick out a pattern of the subtly changing tone, and it gets really annoying.

That's what this felt like. My brain was suddenly picking out a pattern, a sort of rhythm, to the white noise.

Even though I hadn't heard it when I fell asleep.

The longer I lay there, tossing and turning, the more my brain picked up on the pattern. A series of whooshes and clicks. It was really annoying—I'm one of those people who can't sleep in the same room with a ticking clock, and that's what this felt like. *Whooosh. Wup. Click.*

Whooosh. Wup. Click.

My nerves grew ragged.

Whooosh. Wup. Click.

Just when I couldn't stand it anymore—just when I was about to get out of bed and turn it off, because *anything,* even barking dogs at 6 AM, was better than this—I heard it.

A growling sound.

"Who's there?" I shouted.

Nothing.

I sat up—and my heart dropped.

A pair of white eyes floated in the darkness.

On my computer screen.

I watched, frozen, as the eyes shifted—*off* the computer screen. They hung in the darkness a full foot away, staring me down.

Then it moved.

The eyes blazed white as the *thing* leapt for me, shadowy hands reaching across the bed—a shock of pain as something tightened around my wrist—

I scrambled away, kicking. Grabbed my phone off the nightstand, turned on the flashlight.

Nothing was there.

I ran to the door and turned on the lights. The bedroom was empty. I grabbed the laptop—and saw that I was just past the 6:18 mark in the video. The most replayed part.

I rewound it, replayed it.

Nothing was there.

No growl.

No shadowy figure.

No blazing white eyes.

I ran to the bathroom and splashed water on my face, trying to calm myself, to break myself out of the panic. *It was just a dream. You were half asleep. That's all it was.*

But when I looked down at my arm—

I saw a purple bruise just above my wrist.

In the shape of a slender, skeletal hand.

I GOT LOST IN A CORN MAZE

It was the first Saturday of October, and my boyfriend and I found ourselves at the entrance to *Twilight Creek Farm's A-MAZE-ING CORN MAZE!*

It was around 4 pm, and the sun had begun to dip towards the horizon. The air had that crisp autumn chill, hinting at a cold night. A cardboard cut-out stood at the entrance of a cartoony ear of corn, grinning widely.

Yes, it was clear that the intended demographic for this maze was about two decades younger than us.

"Are you sure you want to do this?" Tyler asked.

"Come on, it'll be fun!" I replied, grabbing a map from the anthropomorphized corn. Then I linked my arm with his, and the two of us walked into the maze.

The corn rose up all around us, about seven feet

tall—maybe taller. Our feet sunk slightly into the muddy ground. In retrospect, it probably wasn't a great idea to go corn maze-ing after such a heavy rain. But whatever. We were here now.

The corn quickly swallowed us up. Within a minute, I could no longer see the entrance. Just corn stretching in every direction, a dense forest, choking out all else.

As we rounded the bend, the path ended in a T. There was a metal sign, eroded at the edges, planted firmly in the muddy soil, featuring the cartoon corn again:

Remember these tips to ensure a fun time at our A-MAZE-ING CORN MAZE!

First—Ssshhh, don't tell secrets in the maze! The corn has ears! ;)

Second—Don't stay in the maze after dark!

Third—If you're under 13 years old, stay with your parent or caregiver at all times, please.

And finally: remember, there are no mirrors in the corn maze!

At the bottom of the sign, there were two arrows, and it read:

<— **EASY KIDS' MAZE (EST. 20 MINS)** ... **CHALLENGING MAZE (EST. 1 HOUR)** —>

"Can we just do the kids' maze?" Tyler asked. "It's kind of cold."

"Yeah, but it's so lame," I replied, looking over the map. "It's like, literally a straight line."

He sighed. "Fine."

So we turned right, following the path into the corn. Our footsteps squelched softly in the mud. "So no mirrors in the corn maze?" I asked, trying to start conversation. "What do you think that's supposed to mean?"

He shrugged. "Maybe they want to make it clear it's not like, one of those haunted funhouse things? Like if you see a path, it's real, and not a reflection?"

"I guess."

As we walked down the path, an awkward silence fell over us.

Okay—I'll admit it. I had an ulterior motive for this trip.

Tyler and I had been fighting on and off all week. Just little things, here and there, sniping at each other. It was like something in the air had changed between us. Little things were annoying him, and me, constantly. Maybe it was the shorter days, the lack of sunlight getting to us. Maybe, at almost a year of dating, we were finally coming out of the honeymoon phase. Whatever it was, I felt like a change of scenery would do us some good.

Of course, I was starting to regret that now, with the chill creeping into the air, and the mud sticking to my sneakers. We probably should've just postponed to next weekend, when it wasn't after a heavy rain.

But I felt like I couldn't take one more minute in that apartment.

"Which way now?"

Tyler's voice jerked me out of my thoughts.

I looked up.

Ahead of us, the path split into three—each path considerably narrower than the one we were on.

I looked down at the map.

But I didn't see any places where the path split in three.

"Uh... I don't know."

He raised an eyebrow at me. "We're lost already?"

"Uh..." I looked down at the map again, scanning the schematic. The cartoony ear of corn smiled up at me from the paper, and I wanted to punch it in the face. "I don't see any places where it splits in three," I said, handing him the map.

"Huh," he said, looking over it. "Maybe that's part of the challenge. The map is wrong."

"That'd be kind of interesting."

"Don't they say, if you want to get out of a maze, stick to one side? Like keep your hand touching one wall?" He stretched his arm out and touched the corn on the right.

"Yeah."

I followed him down the rightmost path. It suddenly seemed darker—probably because the path was only about half the width of the previous one, and we were deep in the shadows of the corn. Dry leaves brushed against my arms, feeling more like rough claws, raking against my skin. I felt the cold of the mud permeating through my shoes with each step.

We passed an intersection, and for a split second—out of the corner of my eye—I thought I saw someone walking in the other direction. But when I turned my head, nothing was there.

"I thought I..." I started to Tyler. Then I shook my head. "Nevermind."

Probably just my hair, falling into my line of vision.

Still—I was starting to *really* not like this.

We made another right, and another, following the wall. But we didn't find an exit. More layers of mud caked onto my shoes. I was so tired.

"Maybe we should just turn around and go home," I called out behind him.

He turned around, his eyes lighting up. "Really?"

"Yeah. Should be easy enough to backtrack. We can follow our footprints."

"Sounds good to me," he replied.

We turned around and began to follow our footprints back.

But fifteen or twenty minutes later, we still hadn't found the entrance. *We haven't been here that long. We should be out by now.* "Are you sure we came this way?" I called out, as I followed Tyler down a sharp right turn I didn't remember taking.

"Has to be," he replied, gesturing to our footprints.

But when we turned the corner, we found not one set of our prints, but *two*.

We were going in circles.

"This is ridiculous," Tyler huffed.

"Maybe we should call someone." I pulled out my phone—and my heart dropped. It was 5:23 PM. Over an *hour* since we'd entered the maze.

"What?" Tyler asked, seeing my face drop.

I held up my phone. "We haven't been here this long... have we?"

He paused for a second, then shook his head. "We have to follow our footprints out. We'll get out eventually. And if we're really lost, we can call 911, or something."

"Okay, so which way?" I asked.

One set of footprints went down each path.

"Left. We were making all rights before, so it should be lefts to get out."

We veered left. The corn seemed to squeeze in on us, the path growing narrower with each step. Like the field of corn was some kind of monster, ready to engulf us at any second. I shook my head and continued forward. *There's nothing wrong here. We're just lost in a challenging maze—that's all.*

But when the path widened, I realized how wrong I was.

We were standing in a clearing, about the size of my kitchen. There was a sign, the same battered thin metal as before, in the middle. I froze as I began to read:

There are two ways out of this maze!

You can either find the way out on your own,

Or you can choose to leave behind one person in your party, and the exit will make itself known to you.

Either way... make sure you're out of the maze by nightfall! Because then, nobody makes it out. :)

The cartoon corn-man was painted on the bottom of the sign, grinning up at us. This time, there was a bit of... rust or red paint... around his mouth. I couldn't tell if it was intentional or not. My heart began to pound, I felt like I couldn't get enough air in my lungs, like a panic attack was about to start—

Tyler burst into laughter behind me.

"What?"

"They're trying so hard to make this, like, a scary ARG or something," he said, laughing. "So lame."

I whipped around, arms crossed.

"... You don't actually believe it, do you?"

"All I know is we've been walking around this maze for an hour, but it's only felt like twenty minutes, and the map doesn't match the maze, and I don't remember parts of the maze that we've clearly been to because our footprints are there!" I said, all in one breath. I stared at him, panting, my heart pounding in my chest.

"Kate... I'm sorry... you're really scared, huh?"

"And so are you! I saw how scared you looked when you realized we were going in circles. But now you're just going to pass it off and pretend it's all a game?!"

"Kate..."

"I want to get out of here!" I shouted. "Whatever this is, game or not, I hate it and I want to go home!"

Tyler put up his hands defensively. "Woah, okay, I'm sorry. Let's just keep going left. We'll get out. I promise."

Huffing, I cut in front of him and veered down the left path, leading the way. My shoes squelched loudly. The path narrowed again, corn clawing at my shoulders and hips. We curved left and right—and then, to my relief, the path opened up wider in front of us.

We're out. We're—

The hope leaked out of me like a deflating balloon.

The path did open up into a much larger area. A clearing, like the last one. But I hadn't remembered seeing the clearing—despite footprints trailing all over it.

Our footprints. Crisscrossing, frantic, some clearly made by us running. The depressions in the mud deep and smudged. I turned around—

No.

Tyler wasn't behind me.

My legs went weak underneath me. "Tyler!" I shouted.

The path curved behind me, disappearing into the darkness. No sign of Tyler. I scanned the corn surrounding the clearing—but it was dark and shadowy and infinite, stretching in every direction.

"Tyler!"

The corn rustled, somewhere to my left. I glanced over—but I couldn't see anything. The corn was too dense. The shadows too dark. The sky was darkening now, threatening dusk. It was nearly pitch black in the shadows of the cornfield.

I stared at the mess of footprints on the ground.

What the hell is going on?

I pulled out my phone and called Tyler. It rang several times, then voicemail picked up. "Fuck." I called him a second time, and a third.

He didn't pick up.

For a while I just stood there, calling his name. The sky deepened to dark blue above me. The corn rustled in the breeze, stretching in every direction.

Birds soared to their nests, chirping; then the chittering of bats overhead filled the silence.

There were two paths at either end of the clearing—one curving left, one curving right. Now, they were pitch black. Like looking into the deepest of forests, choking out every last bit of light. I turned on my phone's flashlight and swept it down the entrance of each—but nothing appeared to be there. Just stalks and stalks of corn, all lines and shadows overlapping each other.

And then, finally—I heard something.

Somewhere, down the left path—from just out of my view—I heard a soft whimpering sound.

"Tyler?"

A rough whisper. "Kate?"

I approached the path, my heart pounding in my ears. I held the phone out in front of me, lighting up the path. "Tyler?" I whispered.

And then I saw the blood.

The patch of wet and dark, mingling with the mud.

I swept my flashlight over the corn—

The beam of light fell on a bloody hand. Lying in the mud, just a few feet within the corn.

I jerked the flashlight back, revealing an arm, and then Tyler's face.

He was so pale. His eyes were wide. His cheeks were smeared with blood. "Kate," he groaned, a horrible gurgling sound mingling with his voice.

"I'm coming, I'm going to get you out of there—"

I tried to force my way through the corn. But it was impossible—they were planted only six inches, maybe a foot apart—I didn't have the strength to bend or snap them. "Tyler—what happened—"

"I—"

He didn't get the chance to tell me.

I watched in horror as his body began to slide backwards through the corn.

As if something was *dragging* him.

"Tyler!" I screamed.

The sound of cornstalks snapping filled the air.

I frantically shone my flashlight into the corn, sweeping it in every direction. But all I saw was more and more corn, everywhere, filling up every square inch of space.

I ran back through the clearing, back down one of the paths. Pulled out my phone and dialed 911.

"My boyfriend and I are in a corn maze, and he's—he's hurt, I think there might be someone out there, and—"

"Slow down, please," the woman said. "You said you're at a corn maze?" Her tone sounded skeptical.

"Yeah."

"Where?"

"Twilight Creek Farms."

A beat of silence.

"Do you know what the punishment is for

calling emergency services, when there is no emergency?" she asked, her voice sharp.

"... What?"

"Prank calls can put you in jail for a year. Did you know that?"

I stared at the corn, my throat closing. "What? This isn't a prank call! My boyfriend is really hurt! I think someone—"

"Ma'am," she cut off. "Twilight Creek Farms has been closed for three months now. Ever since the bodies were found."

All the air sucked out of my lungs.

"B-bodies?" I croaked.

"We've gotten over two dozen calls since then, claiming that someone's in trouble," she replied, condescendingly. "But the entire farm was razed, since they lost all their money in the wrongful death suit. So what kind of game are you trying to play?"

"I..." I trailed off. "Three... three months?"

"Uh-huh."

"What... what month is it?"

A scoff. "January."

The phone fell from my hands.

This can't be real. I must be dreaming. I wheeled around, the white of my phone's flashlight sweeping over the corn. The path curved away into darkness, deeper into the corn.

I snatched my phone off the ground and walked

back towards the clearing. But it wasn't there. Like the corn had swallowed it up, grown in its place in the span of minutes.

What the fuck is going on here?!

The sound of footsteps jerked me out of my daze.

Squelch.

Getting louder. Coming closer.

Squelch.

I turned the flashlight off and began running in a random direction. I took every left turn, keeping against the left wall of corn, praying I would find an exit. I tried calling 911 again, and again—but no one ever picked up. They must've flagged my number as some sort of prank call.

The farm has to have some safety system in place. They let kids come here! They have to search the maze before they close up for the night! They wouldn't just let people die here!

I stopped to catch my breath. My lungs burned. I couldn't run anymore. I just couldn't. I stood halfway bent over in the middle of a narrow path, the corn impossibly close, sucking in lungful after lungful of icy air.

"Kate."

Tyler's voice. Incredibly quiet, barely a whisper, from somewhere in front of me.

I began running blindly towards him. The path zigzagged left, then right.

And then I saw him.

Tyler was standing at the end of the path, facing away from me. His form illuminated in silver moonlight, the shadows of the corn crisscrossing over his back.

"Tyler!" I whispered.

I ran towards him. But halfway there, I stopped.

Something is wrong.

He wasn't turning around to look at me. Wasn't moving at all.

"Tyler?"

Nothing.

I grabbed my phone and turned on the flashlight. Hands shaking, I lifted it up.

Nonono.

It was wearing his clothes... but it wasn't him.

It was a scarecrow.

Hay poked out of the neckline of his shirt, out of the cuffs of his jeans. His hands were just bunches of hay, girdled with twine. Stray pieces of hay scattered the ground, falling out of his hiking boots.

But wait...

That didn't quite make sense.

Because he had hair.

Undeniably *his* hair, wavy and black.

The gears in my brain spun, trying to figure out what exactly was going on, trying to interpret this *thing* standing in front of me. Stuffed with hay, with his clothes, his *hair*...

And then I realized it.

The body was a scarecrow—

But the head was not.

I could see Tyler's pale ears. The blood dripping onto the hay of his neck.

I opened my mouth to scream—

The corn stalks rustled and snapped, shaking violently as something moved within them. And then it emerged.

A scarecrow. Moving in jerky, stilted movements, towards me. Holding a long silver blade dripping with blood.

Missing a head.

I took off down the path. My feet pounded underneath me. My lungs burned. I tried to keep right—*because I'd been going left the other way, did that even make sense?*—but everything blurred and smeared in my mind. All I saw was corn, endless rows of it, lit by the moonlight. Pitch black shadows underneath it. A silver moon hanging overhead. Bats twirling and tilting through the air.

After what felt like hours of running, I finally accepted my fate.

I'm never getting out of here.

And neither is Tyler.

Somehow, I evaded the scarecrow all night. Before I knew it, the sun was rising. I thought I'd finally found salvation when I heard voices on the other side of the corn. But then I realized what they were saying:

"*Are you sure you want to do this?*"

"*Come on, it'll be fun!*"

It was *our* voices.

I screamed until I was hoarse, telling them—*us?*—to stay away. I screamed for help. I tried everything. I clawed my way through the corn, towards where I'd heard them—because clearly they were at the entrance—but all I found was more and more corn.

It was futile.

At one point I think I broke through for just an instant—but then I watched her shake her head and say, "Nevermind."

Time passes strangely here, with all our days in the cornfield overlapping each other. Rows upon rows of our footprints cross the dirt, from an eternity of running from the scarecrow. Every time I try to stop Tyler from getting taken, and every time I fail.

And then there's always the night.

I spend every night evading the headless scarecrow. I know my own fate—I know it was bod*ies,* not a body, that was found at the cornfield. I know I don't make it out alive. But I evade her anyway, hiding in the corn, deluding myself that if I stay alive long enough, maybe I will get out.

I'm sure it's been more than three months now,

but the moon rises all the same, hanging silver over the corn. The stalks rustle and snap. I hide in the corn, my breathing fast and heavy, praying that one day I will find a way out.

    I know that day will never come.

I WORK AT THE LAST BLOCKBUSTER IN THE WORLD

Most people think that all Blockbusters went out of business long ago. But I know there's a single store left. It's in the middle of a mostly-abandoned strip mall, among other forgotten relics of the '90s and early 2000s. A pizza place, an arcade, a laundromat. Tattered "For Lease" signs hang in their dusty windows, and mice skitter in the shadows. But the Blockbuster is still there: shelves of shiny DVDs, movie posters tacked on the walls, golden lights spilling out into the empty parking lot.

    I only started working there because they were offering a much higher wage than the rest of the stores around. But right away, I could tell that something was... off. I almost got the feeling it was some sort of Blockbuster rip-off. The sign was the classic blue movie ticket, but the font they used was a little different, and the shade of blue was just a hair too dark. Or, I guess it could've been a new logo Blockbuster created before going out of business? Either way, I could tell something was a little off from the very first time I approached the store.

I'd be working the overnight shift on weekends. This was, according to the manager, the most popular time for the store. "We have a lot of teenagers coming in late at night," Bob told me, "picking up DVDs for parties and dates and whatever."

"Do they not know what Netflix is?" I asked with a laugh.

He didn't reply. Instead, he pulled a folded piece of paper out of his pocket.

"The only thing I ask of you is that you follow these rules. The teenagers can sometimes be a little rowdy, and I want to make sure that my store stays clean and safe."

He handed me the paper and then walked out, leaving me all alone for my first shift.

Nine times out of ten, I probably wouldn't have even looked at the list of rules. It's like reading the terms and conditions before downloading an app—who does that? But something about the tone of his voice, the way he looked at me, made me think this was serious business.

So I got settled behind the counter and unfolded the page. In dated Times New Roman font, there were six rules listed.

1. **You may have one snack from the candy area during your shift, free of charge. We want you to know that you are appreciated here!**
2. **We do not stock a movie called "House of Bones." If you see it anywhere in the store, dispose of it immediately. Do not, under any circumstances, rent it out or watch it yourself. This is an ongoing prank by the local teenagers.**

I raised an eyebrow as I read that rule. *This town's got some pretty creative teenagers,* I thought. What happened to TP'ing houses or whoopie cushions? These kids made up a whole fake *movie* to sneak into the Blockbuster?

My smile faded, however, as I read the next rule.

1. **Stay at least two feet away from the return slot at all times.**

Okay. That's weird. I swallowed, imagining some guy with a butcher knife trying to get me through the return slot. Even though I was well out of the two-foot buffer zone, I scooted my chair even further away.

Then I continued reading.

1. **At some point during the night, usually between the hours of 1 AM and 3 AM, one of our regular customers will visit. You will recognize him easily—he is tall and thin and wears an old-style fedora. He will not say anything, but you must get him a copy of** *The Exorcist.* **Do not say a single word to him.**
2. **We do not have a section for movies on the occult.**
3. **If you see a VHS tape with a handwritten label reading "WATCH ME," dispose of it immediately. Do NOT watch the tape. However, if you hear singing at any point during your shift, you must take the "WATCH ME" tape to the break room and watch it: all of it, without moving for the entirety of the film.**

What even is this? I thought, as I put the letter down. I was expecting things like, if the teenagers got too loud, or if someone came in drunk, kick them out. Or sweep the floor, don't give your friends free movies to rent.

This was just... weird.

Really weird.

A chill went down my spine. I glanced out the

window, but what I saw wasn't exactly reassuring. The place was a ghost town. The entire parking lot was empty, except for a few cars at the opposite end, near the liquor store. That was the only place open.

Since there weren't any customers, I pulled out my phone. I'd been sitting there for about a half hour when I heard something behind me.

A loud clattering sound.

There was a movie in the bin. Someone had used the return slot. I reached down to pick it up—and that's when I realized it was the movie the rules had warned me about.

House of Bones.

I let out a little chuckle. So the teenagers had already made their move. It wasn't even ten o'clock yet.

I picked up the DVD. The cover was creepier than I'd pictured. It showed a sprawling mansion on a hill. All the windows were dark, except for one. In that window, there was the silhouette of a tall, thin man with glowing eyes.

Pretty good Photoshop for a bunch of teenagers.

I got up and walked over to the trash bin to dispose of it, as instructed. That's when I heard a rattling sound—from the DVD case.

Like the teenagers had put little rocks or beads in there.

Or bones.

No, that was ridiculous. This was a harmless prank, orchestrated by some bored teenagers with nothing better to do. I dropped the DVD in the trash.

Then I walked over to the window and scanned the parking lot. To my surprise, I didn't see any cars, or any teenagers. There was only my beat-up sedan, glistening under the streetlamps.

I shook my head and went back to my seat, but the silence was unnerving. I decided to get some restocking done. It had to get done, anyway; now was as good a time as any.

I grabbed the returns cart and pushed it towards the empty aisles.

The store was so quiet. No background music playing, and the TV they had on the back wall was off. I remember going to Blockbusters as a kid, and I remembered they'd always play stuff on the TV, so you'd want to rent more movies. It seemed like a missed opportunity to keep the TV off, especially on what Bob had called their busiest night.

It wasn't just the silence, though. The store almost felt like some sort of weird time capsule from the early 2000s. The beige carpet, the aisles of DVDs, the fluorescent lights shining brightly overhead. All the DVDs were fairly old, too; I hadn't see a single movie that came out after 2010. For example, as I returned some kids' movies, I noticed they didn't have any copies of more recent ones like

Frozen, *Inside Out*, or *Encanto*. It seemed to stop at *Cars* and *Wall-E*.

Why would they only stock older movies?

Was it just too hard to find physical DVD copies of the newer ones?

It only got weirder when I made my way back to the counter. On the far wall, under "New Releases," I saw several copies of *Avatar*, *Up*, and *The Hangover*.

Even though those came out ten, fifteen years ago.

I walked over to the new releases display, scanning, looking for any movie that was even remotely recent. But as I did, a chill went down my spine.

The covers of the movies didn't look quite right. The *Avatar* cover featured a blue alien, but it looked different than the Na'vi—its face was more reptilian than cat-like, with glistening black eyes. The cover of *Up* was still a house being lifted by balloons, but the balloons weren't as colorful. It was like they had all been desaturated: balloons that were olive green, muddy gray, blood red.

And Carl's mouth was wide open in an "O," like he was crying out in pain.

I tore my eyes away. Maybe these were alternate covers I hadn't seen before, or maybe they were special ones the Blockbuster had printed out for some reason—I didn't know. Either way, they left me with a bad feeling.

I returned to the counter and found myself

staring out the window. The only place open in the entire strip mall was the liquor store, all the way at the other end. I wished they were right next to me, instead of the abandoned pizza place.

I didn't want to be alone anymore.

I know. I should've been happy, grateful that there wasn't much for me to do. But I found myself wishing that a group of rowdy teenagers would burst through the door. So who cared if they put some copies of *House of Bones* on the shelves, or swiped some candy? There would be someone in here with me. Something to break this awful chill of fear running through my body.

Bob had said it would be crowded, that this was their busiest time—so why was no one here?

I glanced at my phone. Just past ten o'clock. I grabbed my single appointed snack from the snack area, a box of Junior Mints. Then I propped my phone up and started watching *Late Night with the Devil*. Like a normal person, on a streaming app. Not like this weird time capsule of a store.

But it was only a few minutes later when I heard the jingle of bells.

The door swung open. Three teenage girls came in, giggling. Before I could even say, "Welcome to Blockbuster," they were somewhere deep in the aisles.

I turned back to my phone, feeling like a weight had been lifted off my shoulders. There were other living beings in the store! Witnesses! Even if they were obnoxiously loud—they were here!

And just like that, the whole creepy vibe of the store was shattered.

I could hear them all the way on the other end of the store, see their heads poking out from the aisles, hear snippets of their conversation. Relief flooded me. I leaned back in the chair, and since it sounded like they might be here for a while, I pressed PLAY on my phone. It was hard to hear the dialogue over their obnoxiously loud giggling, but I didn't want to turn up the volume on my phone either and be so obviously goofing off. So I just tried to block it out.

About 15 minutes in, however, I realized that I couldn't hear the girls anymore.

Huh. I paused the movie and sat up straighter, scanning the store. It appeared empty.

"Hello?" I called out.

Nothing.

"You guys still here? Can I help you with anything?"

Total silence.

Maybe they left without me noticing. I was pretty engrossed in the movie, after all. Except... it was nearly impossible for the girls to escape without my noticing, because my counter was right next to the exit. How could I have missed three people leaving the store?

Three *loud* people, at that?

I got up and started walking. My stomach twisted. Nothing about this felt right. I checked the comedy aisle, then action, then horror. Nobody was there.

I made my way around the back of the store, and that's when I heard it.

Whispering.

I couldn't make out what was being said, but it was unmistakable. The girls were still here, hanging around, for some reason. And they had to be hiding on purpose—sitting or crouching within the aisles—because the aisles weren't that tall. If they were standing, I'd see the tops of their heads.

More teenagers, pranking me?

But why? That seemed like a pretty lame prank—to spend a Saturday night hiding in a Blockbuster just so you can scare the random guy working there.

"I know you're there," I called out. "I can hear you whispering."

As soon as I spoke, though, the whispers abruptly stopped.

I turned around, scanning the store—just in time to see the top of a head with strawberry blonde hair duck behind the aisle.

What the hell? Were they... playing hide and seek with me?

On one hand, this wasn't my problem. If some 16-year-old girls wanted to hide in the Blockbuster and laugh at me, whatever. As a twenty-five-year-old with overdue bills, that was the least of my problems. On the other hand, however... I had an easy way of finding them. One click of a mouse back at the counter computer would show me all the in-store security feeds.

And it was kind of my job to make sure they weren't stealing videos or ruining stuff.

So I sat back down at the counter and pulled up the security feed. A split screen appeared, showing four feeds around the store, in grainy black and white. I scanned the aisles, looking for them.

I froze.

There was a girl crouched at the end of the comedy aisle. But where her face should have been, the footage sort of glitched. There was just a black and white smudge there. It immediately reminded me of *The Ring,* and how any character who watched the cursed video showed up with a glitchy face in photos and video.

What the hell?

I decided now would be an excellent time to take a break. I ran to the break room, shut the door, and wedged a chair against it.

This was feeling a lot weirder than some prank pulled off by highschoolers. They wouldn't be able to corrupt the footage like that.

I swallowed and paced the room, my heart pounding.

And then I heard the bells of the front door faintly jingle. They'd left—or maybe someone else had come into the store—but at least I wouldn't be alone with them. So I walked back out, my head on a swivel.

I didn't see anyone, and the store was dead silent.

I breathed a sigh of relief and headed back towards the counter.

That's when I saw it.

Placed on a shelf in the romcom section, between *Bridget Jones's Diary* and *13 Going on 30*, was an old beat-up VHS tape. On the label, in handwritten Sharpie, it read: **WATCH ME.**

Oh, no.

That was one of the videos I had to dispose of.

The girls must have left it here. I would've noticed it before.

I picked it up. Looking at it closer, a chill went down my spine. The label that read **WATCH ME** was new, but poking out from underneath it, I could see the corners of an older label that was stained brown. From dirt or blood or smoke, I didn't know. The plastic windows that showed the rolls of tape had cracks, and the plastic corners of the tape had been warped, as if melted. And darkened, as if scorched.

I swallowed.

Someone tried to burn this tape.

I walked over to the trash can. Without hesitation, I dropped it in. It made a hollow *clunk* at the bottom.

What is going on here?

It wasn't a prank. It was too large-scale for that. The only other thing that came to mind was hazing. Maybe the teenage girls worked here, and they pulled this stuff on every new employee. This was some sort of screwed-up initiation process, a test, where I'd be accepted into their inner circle if I survived the night and didn't run out screaming.

Or something.

I repeated that to myself over and over again for reassurance as I made my way back to the counter.

Whatever it was, I'd obeyed all the rules. I'd thrown out the *House of Bones* movie, I'd thrown out the **WATCH ME** video. Bob really should have warned me more about all of this, though. I didn't sign up for this.

I made it back to my post at the counter, picked up the phone, and started replaying *Late Night with the Devil*. Then I paused it—I was no longer in a horror movie mood. I decided on an episode of *Brooklyn Nine-Nine* instead. That was like, anti-horror, right?

An hour went by without incident. Then another. Gradually, the fear began to fade. Nothing else had happened. Maybe those were all the pranks or hazing or whatever, and it was over. I'd obeyed the rules, I'd passed the test. And here I was, now, earning money watching TV. Maybe this job wasn't so bad, after all.

It was almost midnight when I heard the bells jingle again.

I looked up to see a tall, thin man enter the store. He wore a long black coat that nearly reached his knees and an old-style fedora that kept his eyes in shadow. From his deep wrinkles to his long, knobby fingers, he looked old—far too old to be walking into a Blockbuster. Far too old to stand at a height of roughly six foot six.

All the fear from earlier came back in an instant. *Didn't the rules mention him? Wait, what did they say again?* I reached for the folded paper—but it wasn't there. *Where'd I put it? Oh no, no...*

He walked up to the counter, his footsteps barely making a sound. And then he just... *stared*... at me. Ice-blue eyes that almost looked too bright for being in shadow. Like they were producing their own light. Like they were glowing. The cover of the *House of Bones* movie flashed back through my mind.

I stared up at him, heart pounding.

And then I remembered what I was supposed to do. I couldn't talk to him—I was just supposed to get him a copy of *The Exorcist*. That was it. An easy transaction.

I got up from the counter and walked back

through the aisles. He didn't follow me, but I could feel him watching me. The hairs on the back of my neck stood on end.

I picked up the pace, happy to get rid of this guy as soon as I possibly could.

But rushing was not the right choice. Because, as I walked back towards the counter, I stepped on something. As I slid forward, my arms pinwheeling for balance, I let out a "Woah!"

When I regained my balance, I looked up.

He was closer.

He'd stepped away from the counter, and was now flush with the first aisles of DVDs. He stood perfectly still, head tilted down, eyes glowing slightly in the shadow of his hat. Staring right at me.

Oh, no. Did saying 'woah' when I slipped count as talking to him? But I wasn't talking to him—I was talking to myself—and it wasn't really a word, just an exclamation of surprise—

His mouth stretched into a smile.

And then he took another step.

Nonono. I turned around and sprinted to the break room. The footsteps got louder behind me. Faster. I didn't dare look back.

I burst inside.

Jammed the chair against the door.

I backed away, my heart pounding. Not only

because of the man. But because, as I was running away, I'd seen what I slipped on.

It was the **WATCH ME** tape again.

The tape that I'd just thrown away.

Even though no one had been in the store, someone—some*thing*—had put it in on the floor, in the middle of the aisle.

I stood there, panting. The man's pacing footsteps came through the door. I could see the shadow of his feet from the gap underneath. He was waiting for me to come out. He knew I couldn't stay in here forever.

But I could stay here until the end of my shift.

If only I hadn't left my phone on the counter. Then I could've called the police.

I don't know how much time passed. There wasn't a clock in the room. Maybe an hour, maybe two. But at some point, the footsteps receded, and I heard the familiar jingle of the bells. I waited for a while after that, just to make sure he was gone.

He didn't come back.

When I opened the door, the WATCH ME tape was lying on the ground right in front of me. I picked it up and threw it in the trash again. When I got back to the counter, it was nearly three AM.

I collapsed onto the chair. I could either stay here for the next four hours, and wait for another awful thing to happen... or I could get out.

My car was only fifty feet from the door. Even if the tall man or someone else was out there waiting for me, I'd probably make it. Or maybe my screams would at least be heard by the people at the liquor store. In here—with all the lights on—I was a sitting duck.

I didn't care if I got fired. I didn't care how mad Bob was going to be.

I had to get out.

I got up. Scanned the parking lot, the rest of the strip mall. All clear. Slowly, silently, I walked over to the front door and shoved it open.

Except nothing happened.

I pushed again. And again. I slammed my entire body weight into the thing.

The door didn't budge.

I checked the lock. It wasn't locked.

What the hell?

I ran back over to the counter and grabbed my phone. Dialed 911, not giving too many details, worried they wouldn't believe me. "I'm in the Blockbuster, at the strip mall on Route 54. Please, come as soon as you can," I pleaded.

"The Blockbuster?" the woman repeated.

"Yeah. You know, the one by Reddington Liquor—"

"Sir," she cut in. "The Blockbuster has been closed for fifteen years. Are you saying you broke in?"

All the blood drained out of my face.

"No. I don't... I don't understand."

"They keep the lights on at night, but the store's not open. Did you break in, sir?"

"No... I... just, get someone here, please. I need help."

"An officer's already on their way."

As I hung up the call, I glanced back at the new releases. The rows of *Avatar* and *Up*. Movies that were fifteen years old. Had the store closed, and never been cleaned out? And the lights were kept on all night to deter vandals, but the store wasn't actually open? And Bob—who was he? I'd found his Employees Wanted ad on Nextdoor. Anyone can post there, anyone who claims they live in our general area. What if he was just some random guy? Asking people to stay at the Blockbuster all night?

I sat there, my mind racing, waiting for the police to arrive.

That's when I felt something.

Something grazing my leg.

Something warm.

I looked down—and screamed.

There was a hand, quickly retreating through the return slot. And behind it—a flash of eyes. Pure black. Glistening in the dim light.

And then the thing darted out of sight.

I stumbled away from the return slot. *This can't be happening.* It didn't look human, whatever it was. Eyes pure black... fingers too long... skin that looked patchy and rotted. I looked down at my knee, where it had touched me. There was a thin, pink line from its nail raking against my skin.

I have to get out of here. NOW.

Whatever it takes.

I scanned the room, looking for something heavy. Something that would break glass. The only thing that looked heavy enough to break the glass was the chair I'd been sitting in. I grabbed it, lifted it over the counter, and started towards the door.

I smashed it against the glass.

It began to crack. I lifted the chair and smashed it again.

But then I heard something behind me.

Singing.

I knew what the rules said. To get that **WATCH ME** video and watch it. But I was so close to getting out. Two or three more hits. I bashed the chair into the door again. *CRACK.*

The singing got louder behind me. A woman singing a soft, lilting melody. Shards of glass clattered to the floor.

Almost—

Hands grabbed me from behind.

She yanked me backwards with incredible force. The chair fell from my hands. The singing, in a language I didn't recognize, continued right in my ear. I felt warm breath against the back of my neck.

"Let me go!" I screamed.

I couldn't turn all the way around, from the way she was holding me. But I could see a woman out of the corner of my eye. She had pale skin, strawberry-blonde hair. *The same girl as the teenager earlier?* She was older, though. I could see the gaunt lines of her face, the streaks of silver in her hair.

I screamed again.

She didn't let go.

She continued pulling me back through the aisles, her hands a vice-grip on my shoulders. I frantically scanned the shelves as they went by: horror, action, comedy. And then, finally, I saw it.

On a bottom shelf, next to *The Matrix,* was the **WATCH ME** tape. The rules said all I had to do was watch that video. And I'd be safe.

I thrashed against her grip with all my strength. And for just a second, I slipped out of her grasp. I leapt to the shelf and snatched it up—then ran towards the opposite wall, taking the path to the break room that was farthest away from her.

She scrambled towards me, but the configuration of the aisles slowed her down. I made it to the break room just a second ahead of her, gasping for air.

I barricaded the door and scanned the room. *Is there even a VHS player in here?* I pulled out the drawers of the desk in the room, riffling through them, then headed to the tiny storage closet. And there it was, on a shelf, collecting dust: a VCR underneath an enormous pile of junk.

I slid it out and connected it to the TV, my fingers fumbling over the wires. The singing outside grew louder.

And then it was done.

I slid the VHS tape in and sat down, waiting for it to start.

The image flicked on. Grainy and jumpy, with a date in the upper corner like my old home movies. It read **October 10, 1993**. A cornfield under a blue sky, stalks gently bending in the wind.

I watched, careful not to move, or even shift my weight in the seat. My eyes began to burn. *Am I allowed to blink?* The rules said *don't move for the entirety of the film.* Did blinking count?

I stared at the screen, bright against the darkness of the room.

The scene changed. A field of pumpkins, long past their ideal picking time. Several of them split open and rotting. Dried vines cutting across the dirt. For a second, nothing happened; and then two people came into view. A woman and a child. Both had strawberry blonde hair.

The little girl pointed at one of the rotted pumpkins. The mother shook her head.

Then the mother walked over to the right side of the field and pointed. There was a grainy, dark shape on the ground—a dead bird?

The mother leaned down to scoop it up.

My eyes were watering. Burning. The itch to blink was incredibly strong. I continued to keep them open. I wasn't going to risk it. Behind me, the singing grew softer. Slower. Like the woman on the other side of the door was placated by me watching the video.

The mother carried the dead bird off in her arms, the little girl following after her. Then the video cut to a new scene.

An old bedroom. Decorated in the style of the '60s or '70s, with wooden trim and floral wallpaper. A four-post bed in dark cherry wood stood in the center, with a quilt laid over it.

There was just one problem: there was something under the quilt.

It looked like a body.

Footsteps approached. And then a girl appeared on screen, wearing an ankle-length floral dress. She looked like she was in her teens, with the same strawberry blonde hair. A ginger tabby cat followed in her footsteps.

I couldn't see her face, but it looked like the girl who was hiding in the aisles of the Blockbuster earlier.

She knelt beside the bed, beside the body, facing away from me. I thought I heard her voice, but the tape was too corrupted to make out the words. Then, a few seconds later, she got up and left the room.

As I stared at the screen, I realized there was a lock of strawberry blonde hair peeking out from under the edge of the quilt.

As the camera lingered on the body, I felt the incredible urge to blink. My eyes felt like they were on fire. Watering, a tear rolling down my cheek.

There's no way blinking counts as movement. Right? I asked myself.

I *had* to blink. I had to. It hurt so much.

Hold out for a little longer, I told myself. *Come on, hold out, please...*

But the pain was too much.

I blinked. Relief flooded me when nothing happened. I blinked again, tears running down my cheeks.

Careful to keep the rest of my body absolutely frozen, I continued watching.

The scene changed again. Well, it didn't really *change*—it was the same room, with the body under the quilt. But the lighting from the windows had changed, and the folds on the blanket had also changed. I couldn't tell how much time had passed from the previous shot. Was it later the same day? Or weeks, or months, later?

The girl came in again. She was holding a burlap bag. She spilled it onto the floor, and I couldn't see much, with the quality of the film—but I could make out black feathers and a few candles.

She began lining the feathers around the bed, around the body, and lighting each of the candles. She then knelt at the bed again, still facing away from me. Almost like she was intentionally never letting the camera see her face.

What is this?

A videotape of some demonic ritual?

As I sat there, watching, the audio cut in.

The girl on the tape wasn't talking, wasn't chanting, as she knelt at her mother's bedside. She was *singing*.

The same song, in the same unrecognizable language, as the woman outside the door. And as she sang, I realized I heard two voices. But the second voice wasn't coming from behind me—it was coming from the TV speakers.

The dead body was singing.

The shape under the blanket began to move. I watched in horror as it started to sit up. The quilt began to fall from her face—

The video cut out with a flash of black-and-white static.

And then the next scene. The woods. Trees jutting up on either side, stretching into the darkening sky. Two women stood in the middle of a clearing, their backs to the camera. With long, strawberry blonde hair.

It took me a minute to realize they were dragging something behind them. The footage was too grainy to tell what it was. But I had a pretty good idea, as soon as they grabbed the shovels leaned against the trees. The sounds of steel cutting into earth and soil hitting the ground was unmistakable.

They were burying a body.

These women... were they bringing things back from the dead? It was the only thing that made even the faintest bit of sense. A dead bird, a live cat. A dead person, buried in the woods, and a live mother. But why would they videotape it?

And why would watching it protect me?

I guess the rules never really said it would protect me. The rules just told me to watch it. I swallowed, staring at the grainy image of the dark woods. *How much longer does this video go on? The police should be here by now.*

But the store behind me was silent.

The camera began zooming in on the two women digging into the earth. And when it got close enough to see the women's faces, I realized I couldn't see them. Their faces were just grainy smudges of color. Just like the teenage girl on the security camera.

The video then glitched again, black and white snow—and then it cut to a view of the grave and the body.

My heart dropped to the floor.

The dead body... looked exactly like *me*.

Even though the rest of the film was grainy, my

face was perfectly clear. It was like the tape had somehow supernaturally captured my likeness and pasted it onto the body in the film. I could make out a thin layer of stubble, the birthmark under my right eye. My eyes were closed, my face was deathly pale, and my mouth hung open slightly.

I was dead.

The camera suddenly flipped up to show the two women. Even though their faces were only smudges of color, I felt like they were smiling. I felt like I could feel their evil, oozing through the screen. My entire body felt cold.

There was one last scene to the tape.

I recognized the place on the screen instantly. It was the inside of the Blockbuster, from years ago: the place was bustling. Groups of teenagers, families with small children, couples holding hands all walked up and down the aisles, perusing the shelves.

Close to the camera, the daughter stepped into the frame. She paused, pulled a VHS tape out of her purse, and left it on the shelf.

The tape read, in bold, black letters: **WATCH ME.**

The video finally stopped. A *click* and a rolling sound, as the tape self-ejected. As soon as it did, there was an explosion of sound in my ears. Someone was pounding on the door behind me. Shouting: "Police! Open up!"

It was like I'd been underwater, and suddenly brought to the surface. Like I'd been in a trance, that was now broken.

I pulled the chair away and opened the door. Two officers stood on the other side, shining a flashlight in my face. Strangely, behind them, the Blockbuster was dark.

"We've been banging on the door for a good five minutes," one of them said. "What the hell are you doing in here?"

I glanced back at the TV. The screen was black. And... strangely... there was no VHS tape sticking out of the VCR.

"There was this woman... and a tape..." I tried to explain, feebly.

I told them everything. But they didn't believe a word of it. In fact, they thought I was vandalizing the place. That *I* was the villain here. The official report said I was arrested for vandalism. That I'd stolen a box of Junior Mints and broken a front door at a defunct Blockbuster.

My manager "Bob"—if that was even his real name—was never found.

I had to pay a hefty fine and do some community service, but otherwise, there were no consequences from the incident.

Except for one.

Last night, when I was doing some cleaning, I found a VHS tape wedged between some old home videos in the basement. In bold letters, it read: **WATCH ME.**

I've thrown it out three times now. And I've refound it somewhere else in my house every time. On my bookshelf. On the kitchen table. In my closet.

WATCH ME.

And last night, when I looked out the window—I saw two women standing in my backyard, at the edge of the forest. Reddish hair falling over their shoulders. Faces that were only smudges of color.

They were holding hands.

Staring up at my window.

The rules never promised I'd be safe. They told me not to watch the video, unless I heard singing. Maybe watching the video was a last resort. Maybe it just bought me time. How much time? A few months? A year?

Tonight, I found the tape again. It was under my bed.

And as I look out the window, I see two figures standing in my backyard.

They're getting closer.

I LET MY SON USE THE COPIER

I think we've all put our faces in copiers as kids. It was a fun thing to do, especially when we didn't have modern luxuries like iPads or YouTube.

So yesterday afternoon, when my kid was bored as heck, I decided to give it a try with him.

Yeah, it was a waste of ink. But honestly, it was worth it, if it pried my kid away from Minecraft speed runs and hot wheels unboxing videos. I switched it to black-and-white ink only, and started the fun.

We copied his hands a few times. He laughed with glee. "Do your face now," I told him. He scrunched his lips up, like an exaggerated duck face, and stuck his face against the glass. I lowered the lid on his head (which was very light.)

"Close your eyes! The light's bright!" I told him,

as the band of white light began sliding across the glass, scanning his face.

Then came the *ch-ch-ch* of the page printing.

But when he grabbed the page, my heart sank.

In the picture... his eyes were open. He wasn't doing the duck face, either.

"Did you open your eyes?" I asked him.

He shook his head.

I stared down at the picture. His face pressed up against the glass, his cheeks and forehead pushed flat. In the high contrast, his medium-brown eyes looked pure black.

"Again! Again!" Matthew chanted, lifting the lid and sticking his head in.

I hesitated. Then I lowered the lid and pressed copy.

Ch-ch-ch.

The paper came out, inch by inch.

I saw Matthew's ear.

Then his cheek.

His eye—wide open.

And then his mouth.

His mouth stretched out into a gaping O. As if he were screaming.

I grabbed Matthew and pulled him back. The lid clattered shut. "But it's not done!" he protested.

Ch-ch-ch—the rest of the page came out, although I could see the exact moment I'd pulled Matthew away. There was a line three-quarters of the way across his face, cutting off half his right eye and cheek, turning into a mess of warped gray lines.

"Does this scare you?" I asked.

"No."

"I think we should play with something else for a while," I said.

"But I want to do this!"

I was finally able to pull him away from it and give him something else to do. But even after he was in bed that night, something disturbed me. While the copies were being made, I could see his face under the lid. The second time, I'd stared at his face the entire time, to make sure he didn't open his eyes.

He didn't.

So why did the picture show his eyes open?

I told my husband about the whole thing after Matthew was asleep. "Hey, I remember doing that when I was a kid," Peter laughed. "I remember doing my butt, too. I got in a lot of trouble for that."

"But... I swear he didn't open his eyes."

"He probably did for just a second."

But if he'd only opened his eyes for a second... The scanner moved linearly, printing as it copied. If he'd opened his eyes just for a second, I'd expect to see one eye open and one eye closed, or even just half an eye open. When I'd pulled his head away, the rest of his head didn't copy.

I explained this all to him, but he was unperturbed. "Let me try it," he said.

"... What?"

"Might just be a glitch or something."

Peter walked over to the printer and turned it on. Lifted the lid and stuck his face in. The scanner-light hummed to life, sliding across the glass. *Ch-ch-ch*—the page began to print.

And then it happened.

I noticed the page first. My husband's eye on the page, wide with fear. The corner of his mouth twisting down.

And then he was pulled *into* the printer.

I don't know how else to describe it. It was like something... something under the glass, next to the blinding strip of light... grabbed him by the head and yanked him through. I heard glass shatter.

It happened so fast, by the time I lunged for him, only his feet were poking out.

Then the lid clattered shut, and he was gone.

"Peter?" I screamed. "Peter!"

Ch-ch-ch.

The rest of the page printed out.

Peter's face—his final image—printed on the page. The left side of this face, perfectly clear—eye wide, mouth open. Abject terror.

The other side of his face...

A twisted mess of warped lines, fading into black.

Printed in Great Britain
by Amazon